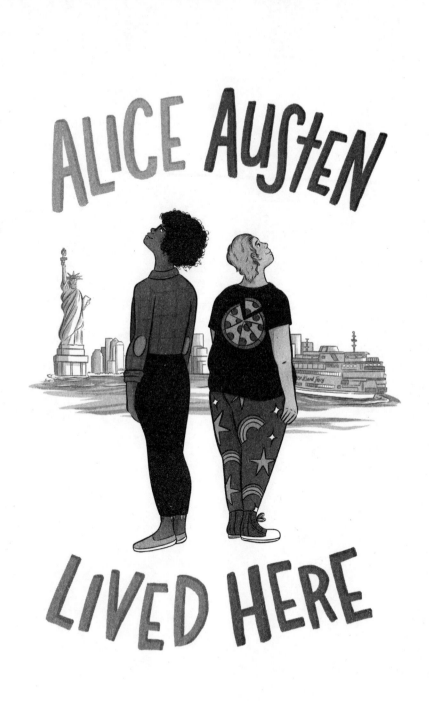

ALSO BY ALEX GINO

Melissa

You Don't Know Everything, Jilly P!

Rick

ALICE AUSTEN LIVED HERE

ALEX GINO

Scholastic Press / New York

Library of Congress Cataloging-in-Publication Data available

ISBN 978-1-338-73389-1

10 9 8 7 6 5 4 3 2 1   22 23 24 25 26

Printed in Italy 183
First edition, April 2022

Book design by Maeve Norton

FOR THE RAINBOW OF PEOPLE
WHO HAVE GOTTEN US HERE,
FOR OUR VIBRANT QUEER AND
TRANS COMMUNITIES NOW,
AND FOR THE INEFFABLE FUTURE.
LANGUAGE CHANGES; THE NEED
TO BE OURSELVES DOESN'T.

CHAPTER ONE

I can see the Statue of Liberty from my bedroom window. I'm not trying to brag. It's just true. My view is of New York Bay, with New Jersey sprawled out on the left side, downtown Manhattan poking up into the sky on the right, and between them, there she is, Lady Liberty. She's not close enough to be able to see her face clearly without binoculars, but she's an unmistakable green spot in the water.

"She has seven spikes on her crown," I told TJ as we lay on my bed one afternoon, leaning our elbows on the windowsill. "Some people say it's to match the seven continents or the seven seas. Other people say it's supposed to be the rays of the sun, but then why would there be seven of them? And she's in the water. It's gotta be the seas."

TJ looked at me with one eyebrow raised and one lowered.

"Since when are you an expert on the Statue of Liberty?"

"Since I watched a video online with Jess."

TJ's dark hair fell onto their forehead in perfect ringlets that barely reached their thick-framed glasses. They wore black jeans and a magenta button-down shirt that brought out the rosy hint of their angular, tan face. As for me, I wore one of my many black T-shirts that Mom said washed out my round, pale face. My dirty-blond-turning-to-brown hair was cut shorter than I would have liked, the effects of an unpleasant gender experiment that I was still waiting to grow out. My shirt was from Joe & Pat's, hands down the best pizza place on Staten Island. According to my hands anyway. TJ's family swore by Nunzio's.

We lived on Staten Island, the forgotten borough of New York City. Staten Island is nearly the size of Brooklyn, but with one-fifth the population. Home of the Verrazzano-Narrows Bridge, the minor league Yankees, and, of course, the Staten Island Ferry. In other words, a place known for ways to leave it. And if you've ever seen a map of New York where there's a little bump in the bottom-left corner that the mapmaker didn't bother drawing the rest of—just enough to let the ferry dock before it heads back to Manhattan—that's the little bit of Staten Island we lived on.

"Okay. If you know everything about the Statue of Liberty, which hand is the book in?" TJ asked.

"Easy. Her left."

"Are you *sure*?"

"One hundred percent."

"But how can you *know*?"

"Because she's holding the torch with her right."

"You're good! Most people get tripped up when you ask them about details like that. I'll bet my dad doesn't even know." TJ's dad was a trivia buff as well as a professional chef.

"Yeah, well, your dad doesn't have a personal view."

TJ's family lived in a house a block away, and their bedroom view was of their backyard, a patchy green square with a large oak tree filling up the center. My building was five stories tall, plus a basement, so technically, we lived in a penthouse, but really, it was just a regular two-bedroom apartment in an old brick building—141 St. Mark's Place. Apartment 5-C. I hadn't been able to say my address without it singsonging out of my mouth ever since I was little and had to memorize it along with Mom's cell phone number just in case I got lost. *ONE-forty-onnnnne, ST.! MARK'S! PLACE! a-PART-ment, FIIIIVE CEEEEE.*

I told TJ more of what I'd learned. "There are three hundred fifty-four steps up to the top. Well, to her crown anyway. No one's been allowed to climb to the top of the torch since she got hit with shrapnel from an explosion around World War I."

"Why do you keep calling them *she* anyway? How do you know what pronouns a statue uses?" TJ is the only person I know who's more careful about pronouns than I am.

"Well, she is called *Lady* Liberty," I pointed out.

"Not all ladies are women."

"True, they could be a nonbinary drag queen! They are wearing a tiara, after all."

"Now *that* would be amazing!" TJ stood and put my baseball hat on their head, with the bill popped up. They grabbed a unicorn coloring book to hold in their left arm and raised a pencil in their right. "No puny gender can hold me back! I am no mere man or woman. I am Mx. Liberty, and I light the way for you!"

TJ and I were the only nonbinary kids in our grade—at least as far as we knew. That's not why we were best friends, and being best friends wasn't why we were both enby, no matter what TJ's grandmother thought. It was just one of many things we had in common. We both lived on the same street, loved graphic novels, and thought the pop star Miss Chris was the coolest ever. We always had something to talk about, and when we didn't, our silence was the comfortable kind. We loved to make boxed mac 'n' cheese together (gluten-free because TJ was allergic to wheat) and eat it with tiny fish forks in candlelight, pretending it was the fanciest item on the menu at the chichiest French restaurant. We were even both born in October, and the previous year, we'd had a combination Halloween birthday party in TJ's backyard.

My phone barked. Technically, it was the alarm set to a barking ringtone, but either way, it was dog-walking time. The pug, Nacious, lived downstairs with Ms. Hansen, an old woman with short white hair and a friendly laugh. Ms. Hansen gave Nacious her daily walks, but TJ and I were responsible for taking her out on Sundays to really tire her out.

"Ready?" I asked TJ, who jumped up in response. They liked Nacious more than I did. TJ loved all dogs, even the big and growly ones. They said it was all in the eyes. I said I was a cat person, but I made exceptions, especially for dogs like Nacious who weren't very doglike at all.

We raced down the stairs to Ms. Hansen's first-floor apartment. Ms. Hansen didn't have a view of the Statue of Liberty, since her windows were too close to the ground to see the water. All she could see was the back of the building behind us.

Ms. Hansen met us at the door with Nacious already on her leash. We grabbed some tennis balls and set out down the block for the yard next to the stone church, with its hill that we made Nacious run up and down as we tossed the tennis ball at each other. Neither of us had very good aim, but luckily, Nacious liked to run after the ball and bring it back to TJ for tug-of-war. She knew not to bring it to me. Maybe she was happy. Or maybe she was frustrated. It was hard to say. Like I said, I wasn't really a dog person.

We walked back to 141 St. Mark's Place with Nacious. I knew every crack in the walkway to the entrance, the musty smell of the mailbox area in the outer lobby, and the number of stairs between each floor. I thought I knew a lot about the place, but I had no idea there was history to be discovered.

And not just any history. Queer history.

CHAPTER TWO

My life wasn't too bad, really. Seventh grade was awful, but Jess said that anyone who didn't think middle school was awful wasn't to be trusted. Jess was my other best friend. She lived one floor down, in apartment 4-E, with her partner, Val, and their baby, Evie. Jess was femme, Val was nonbinary, and they were both queer.

On Tuesdays after school, I "babysat" Evie. It wasn't *really* babysitting because Jess stayed there, and it wasn't like I got paid. But Jess appreciated the help, and I got to hang out with two of the coolest people I knew. Three, if you counted Val, who usually got home from work a few minutes before the end of my "shift."

Today was Val's birthday, so I was extra eager to get downstairs. Jess was waiting on me to entertain Evie so she could frost the cake.

"I'll be back a little late," I told Mom, who was on the couch, typing on the laptop propped across her legs.

"Oh?"

"I'm staying for cake!"

"Cake before dinner?"

"I'm living on the wild side?" I gave my best I-love-you-and-I-also-love-cake grin.

"Fine," said Mom. "Wish Val a happy birthday for me. How old are they now?"

"Twenty-five!"

"And Jess is?"

"Twenty-eight."

Mom pursed her lips for a moment before speaking. "Sam, how many kids do you think have friends more than twice their age?"

"Well, Evie is my friend too, and she's only six months old, so on average, they're more like seventeen," I replied. I'm good with numbers.

"Closer to eighteen." Mom was good with numbers too.

"I'm spending time with a newborn and her family. Most parents would be delighted to see their kid being so helpful."

Mom raised an eyebrow. "Fair point. Go ahead. I could use a little peace and quiet. I don't know how Jess bears with you *and* Evie."

"I love you!" I pulled on my fuzzy green slippers and ran down to the fourth floor.

Jess had left the apartment door unlocked for me, so I let myself in and dropped my slippers by the door. If the stairs hadn't been so dirty, I would have just come down in socks, but Jess had threatened to make me wash the floors of their apartment if I did, so slippers it was.

Jess was on the couch, scrolling on her phone, jet-black hair framing her round peach-white face. Evie was in her lap, chewing on her baby fist.

"Hey, Sam!" Jess said when she saw me. "Want to take the sack?"

Jess and Val sometimes called Evie a *sack* as in a *sack of potatoes*. I had tried lifting a bag of potatoes and found it to be lighter than Evie, and way less wiggly. Evie was more like a pillowcase of worms, but that didn't catch on as a nickname.

"Sure," I said, picking up Evie and then sitting down on the floor with her. I put a finger into each of her fists and wiggle-danced along with her and the punk music in the background.

"I'm about ready to frost the cake. I just need to get changed first." Jess was wearing a black T-shirt and pink leggings, but she liked to dress up when she baked. She came back wearing red lipstick and a full-length red gingham apron over an electric-blue dress with a short flared skirt.

Jess had taught me that being femme wasn't the same as being a woman. In fact, plenty of femmes weren't women. It wasn't even the same as being feminine. Jess said that only you can name yourself as femme and that you get to make it yours. Lots of straight women dress and act the ways some people expect women to. Sometimes they enjoy it, but sometimes they do it to fit in at work or to get dates. But if you choose to do it because it makes you feel good, and you make it queer, like by wearing a fancy dress to bake a birthday cake for your nonbinary partner, it's femme.

I was amazed that Jess never got flour on her, not even on the apron. She barely even spilled any on the counter. She turned up the riot grrrls on the speakers around the room, who wanted to know *who invited you?* Then she plugged in her ruby-red stand mixer next to the powdered sugar, butter, and cream cheese ready to be whipped into tasty pillows of frosting.

This was the first cake Jess had made since Evie's birth almost six months ago. Before Evie, there hadn't been a week that Jess didn't have a cake or cookie or pie to share. In fact, the offer of baked goods had first brought me to Jess and Val's place six years ago. Mom and I had met them in the lobby, waiting for the elevator. They had moved in the week before, and they invited us over for slices of tres leches cake.

The next week it was an apple galette. The week after that? Snickerdoodles.

Pretty soon, it was just me heading downstairs, feasting on sweet treats and conversations about queer theory and riot grrrls and fat activism and a thousand other things Mom didn't know anything about. Mom was pretty cool . . . for a self-identified straight person. I was four when I first told her I wasn't a boy or a girl, and she read books and watched videos and even got my pronouns right almost every time. But it was Jess and I who talked about queer culture, not to mention being fat and fabulous.

Jess dumped butter into the mixer bowl, dropped the heavy arm, and locked the beater into place. With a click, she started the mixer at its slowest, growliest setting. She raised the speed until the warbling pitch of the motor rose to a steady hum, then tipped a cup of powdered sugar over the mixer, shaking in an even, powdery stream. I was amazed how little sugar puffed up. When I'd tried adding powdered sugar into a moving mixer, it was like creating a kitchen-sized snow globe.

"It's so good to be baking," Jess said, pulling the spice cake out of the fridge while the beaters cut air into the frosting mixture. "I finally have enough energy to do something other than keeping Evie fed and clean, and it feels good to be back in my element." She picked a large knife off a metal strip on the wall, bent down to the level of the cake, and carefully sliced off the dome in the center so she'd have a flat surface to frost.

She brought a plate of trimmings out to share. I mashed a handful in my hand and popped it into my mouth. The spice cake was soft and smelled like warm, cinnamony heaven.

"I'm glad you're here to keep Evie occupied. I'm sure I could manage by myself, but it's been a while since I've frosted a cake, and I want to be able to concentrate."

"Well, you're still really good at the baking part!" I took another handful.

"I'm glad you think so. I had to keep rereading the recipe to make sure I hadn't forgotten anything. Okay, back to the frost!"

"Wait!" I cried, standing up.

"What?" Jess asked.

"This cake deserves a belly bump!"

Jess and I had given each other belly bumps since she first taught them to me when I was in fourth grade. I had been feeling bad about my body, and said that I wished that I was thin like TJ. She took me in front of a mirror and made me say three nice things about my body. She did it too. Stuff like *I really like my shoulders* and *Thank you, legs, for carrying me around*. And then we did our very first belly bump.

I had been shorter then, so she got down on her knees. Then we both raised our shirts so that an inch of our stomachs showed, and we pressed them together, skin right on warm skin. "Belly power!" we had yelled.

And "belly power!" was what we cried before Jess went back to the kitchen to finish Val's birthday cake.

She turned off the mixer, and soon she had piping bags that she used like pink, blue, purple, and green paint to create sugary flowers and leaves with deft turns and flicks of her wrist. When she was done, the cake looked like a garden in full bloom.

"Wow times a million!" I exclaimed.

Jess had taught me how to pipe flowers onto cupcakes, so I knew how hard it was. Or at least she'd tried to teach me. I'd ended up with three unpleasant roundish blobs and nine unpleasant oblong blobs, which was when I decided that I would rather eat dessert than decorate it.

"There are exactly twenty-five flowers," Jess announced proudly.

"Cool! One for every year Val's been alive."

"You got it!" She put a glass cover over the cake and turned up the music. "The louder the jams, the easier the cleanup. Also, some company never hurt."

After a smile and a wink, she picked up Evie and buckled her into her bouncer seat. I joined Jess in the kitchen to put away ingredients, wipe down surfaces, and tackle the heap of dishes in the sink. Then we rewarded ourselves with a punk dance party in the living room. Jess carried Evie on one hip while twirling me around and around with her other hand. Every once in a while, Jess would switch directions so that I wouldn't get dizzy. I'm not sure it helped, because I ended up pretty wobbly anyway.

Evie was back in her bouncer seat, but Jess and I were still zombie dancing to "Pretend We're Dead" by L7 when Val came home. They kicked off their loafers, tossed their hat onto the back of the couch, and joined in. They were short and round, from their wavy black hair to their dimpled copper-brown cheeks to their sizable belly, and they wore khakis and a blue-and-black checkerboard vest over a light blue button-down shirt. With their hands above their head, they shook their hips with the joy of someone who loves their body. Then they slowly took off their vest, taking a step toward Jess with each button and slipping it off with a quick tug and a shake of their shoulders. They met Jess with a kiss that went on so long I had to look away.

When they were done, Jess said, "Hey there, Birthday Queer. I made you somethin'." She tossed her head in the direction of the kitchen.

"Cake?" they asked, eyebrows high.

Jess smiled and posed her hands below her chin to frame her face.

"Cake!" Val repeated with confidence. They ran to the kitchen. "CAKE!"

"Candles?" Jess offered, but Val shook their head.

"CAKE!" They pointed to their mouth as a hint to where they wanted the cake to be.

"Can we at least sing first?"

"CAKE!!!" Val took a knife, pointed the tip at the center flower, and brought the handle down and through the soft sponge.

"Wait wait wait," said Jess. "It's bad luck to pull out the knife of your own birthday cake."

"Says who?" Val crinkled their face but let Jess take over.

"Nice to see you can say words other than *cake*." Jess positioned the knife to cut out the first slice.

"Cake now! Cake!" Val pointed at their mouth with an even more exaggerated gesture.

"Really?" Jess's eyebrows lifted in mock annoyance.

"Cake cake cake cake cake!!!" Val pulled a fork from the dish rack and banged it on the counter.

Jess's pretend irritation looked ready to spill over to the real thing. Val stopped banging the fork.

"Puh-leeeeeease?" They drew out the word, batting their eyelashes the whole time.

"I love you, you goofus." Jess laughed as she spoke, and handed them the first slice of cake.

They placed a bite in their mouth and sank into a kitchen chair with euphoric ease. "Caaaaaaaake." They took another bite and made more noises of delight. After bite four, they refound words. "Oh, Jess, thank you. This is scrumptious."

"Happy birthday!" said Jess. "I love you."

"I love you too."

"I hate to break the moment," I said, "but, uh" —I pointed my finger at my mouth—"cake?"

Soon, all three of us had slices (Val was on their second) and even Evie got a taste of cream cheese frosting on her tongue. She banged her hands on her high chair tray with delight. She was right—it was fantastic.

"Should we sing now that you have cake?" I asked.

"Nah," said Val. "I don't need all that."

"But twenty-five's a big deal," I pointed out. "You're a quarter of a century old."

"When I was your age, birthdays were everything. I didn't just celebrate my half birthday—I used to celebrate every month. Nothing big, but I would make a sandwich, light a candle on top, sing to myself, and blow it out. I felt so old when I turned thirteen. And fourteen. Fifteen was terrible. Sixteen was okay, but seventeen couldn't finish fast enough. I couldn't wait to turn eighteen. That was a big one. And then it was over and I was on the other side of it and nothing had really changed. No halo on my head or nothin'. After that I was in college and hanging out with people of all sorts of ages, and, I don't know, it just kind of mattered less. I had a huge bash for my twenty-first birthday. But since? I've just been in my *early twenties*."

"Not anymore!" I pointed out.

"True. That's why Jess and I are going out with some friends for drinks this weekend. But other than that, it's just another day."

I almost asked if I could come along, but then I realized that drinks didn't mean soda, and I was glad I'd kept my mouth shut.

Jess cleared her throat with mock indignation. "Well, if it's just another day, maybe I shouldn't have bothered with a cake."

"That," said Val, hugging their plate close to their chest, "is NOT what I'm saying."

I was tempted to eat a second slice, but if I went upstairs too full for dinner, Mom would go on about how she should never have let me go downstairs for cake in the first place, and that was not worth a second slice, especially not when there would still be some left the next afternoon when I visited again.

I gave Evie a squeeze, put my dishes in the sink, and fuzzy slippered my way back upstairs.

CHAPTER THREE

I didn't think I'd ever be the kind of person who didn't "make a fuss" about their birthday, but still, I'd learned a heck of a lot from Jess and Val, and not just about old punk bands. If they'd been my only friends, I might have understood Mom's concern about their age. But I had TJ, who I saw just about every day.

TJ stayed over at my place most weekends that their family was in town. TJ's family was much bigger than mine—they had four siblings while I was an only child, and I had one less parent around. Mom had mostly been single since she broke up with my dad when I was a toddler, and she said she was happier not to worry about dating. Me, I was happy not to have an older brother who teased me when I took a long time in the shower, or a little sister who came in and messed with my things. TJ had both of those, plus an older sister who acted like a third parent, and a baby brother who screamed while TJ was trying to do their homework. An older sister, an older brother, a younger sister, and a younger brother. *One of each*, heteronormative people tend to say. TJ called them the Littles and the Bigs. It was a lot.

If we didn't have so much fun together, I might have thought TJ only stayed over for the chance to take a shower without anyone banging on the door or running a load of laundry that used up all the hot water. But we always had a great time reading graphic novels, listening to music, and talking for hours about everything and nothing. The food wasn't as good as at TJ's—TJ's dad was a chef, after all—but at least you didn't have to fight for the serving spoon.

TJ and I spent most of our time together at school though. Lunch alone was forty-five minutes a day. If you counted the classes we took together, which were almost all of them, we spent about twenty-four hours together at school in a normal week. It wasn't all fun time, which only made it feel longer. And no class was as long as US History with Watras.

The Monday after Val's birthday, TJ and I were groaning that weekends should be at least three days long when the bell rang and Watras clapped his hands. "If you are not in your seat, you are now late." It was funny how the same teachers who declared that "the bell doesn't release you; I do" sure did have a lot of faith in the bell that *started* class. None of our other teachers took attendance, but Watras insisted on beginning each lesson by pulling out his old red attendance binder.

He was a teacher, so technically, he was Mr. Watras, and that's what students said when they talked to him, which they did as little as possible. But when they were talking *about* him? It was just Watras, unchanged since he'd sprouted from the primordial ooze, marking dinosaurs late for not having evolved on time.

After a homework check, Watras launched into a long speech about a bunch of dead rich white guys fighting over how to run the US government after the Revolutionary War. It could have been interesting if Watras wanted to explore the contradiction of saying you fought the British for freedom while having slaves work the land you stole from the Indigenous people who had been here and free for thousands of years before you, but he didn't bring any of that up.

Instead we got twenty of the most boring minutes on record, tied with every other time Watras gave what he called a "traditional lecture," which happened at least twice a week. Everyone was supposed to take notes on "the important parts," but he wouldn't tell us what the important parts were. If you had questions, you had to hold them until he was done "so as not to disturb the flow of the lecture." Even if you were confused. And if, when he was finally done talking, you *did* tell him you were confused, he would either say "I'm about to explain that," or "I've already explained that"—neither of which was helpful.

Traditional lessons usually ended with a "traditional question-and-answer session," and if no one had Qs for him to A, Watras had some of his own to prove that you hadn't been taking good enough notes. This time, Watras wrapped up after three questions, with a full five minutes left in the period. There was a wisp of hope in the air that perhaps he had misread the clock and would release us early.

The wisp dissolved when he said, "Before we end today, I want to let you know about an exciting project we're about to embark on."

Most of us held our groans. A few were less subtle.

"It's popular these days to talk about how we're all different and unique," said Watras.

The word *unique* didn't sound good coming out of his mouth. My stomach gave a twist.

"And we *are*, of course." Watras said this like someone had told him to. "But we all have a commonality." He paused for effect. "We're all . . . New Yorkers."

"Tell that to my cousin Eli from Brooklyn," Josh called out. "He's always saying that New York City is made up of four boroughs and a sidekick."

A few kids laughed, and Abe said, "Brooklyn can bite my—" but the last word was covered up by a loud cough from Watras.

"Interborough squabbles aside, you should all be proud to live in one of the greatest cities in the country, if not the world. And a city that is providing you a rare opportunity, because Borough Hall is commissioning a new statue for the base of its steps to look out on New York Harbor, and the subject for that statue will come from a young Staten Islander."

Cara raised her hand, but Watras waved it down, which was his way of saying that he was going to keep speaking and, as usual, would only take questions when he was done. He clapped his hands together in a rare display of enthusiasm. "Isn't that exciting?"

No one but Watras looked excited.

"I, myself, have a great many ideas for historical figures I would like to see grace the steps of Borough Hall, but the maximum age for entrants is fifteen, and I'm just a shade over that." Watras laughed as if he had just told a joke. He explained that entries needed to include an essay about the local and personal significance of the subject, a proposed statue image, and a letter of recommendation from a teacher.

"So your assignment is to create an entry for this contest . . . and then my assignment will be to write the letter of recommendation for the project that is awarded the highest grade and enter it into the borough-wide competition. Your essay and image will also count as your semester partner project. I expect you to approach this task with the proper reverence and maturity. *No contemporary subjects.*" He looked over the room, as if expecting applause. When none arrived, he said, "Now that I am *done*, are there any questions?"

Cara raised her hand again before asking, "What do you mean, a subject? Like a math statue or something?"

Watras shook his head. "Can anyone explain to Miss Zimmerman what I mean by *subject*?"

"Like a person or whatever," said Liz.

"Not *like* a person." Watras huffed with the exasperation of someone who has been bothered by inanity too many times to be surprised but isn't willing to let said inanity pass without note. "A subject *is* a person. In this case, a figure of local note. And no, not a note like you pass in class, Cara. I speak of a person of distinction. Someone who is meaningful to Staten Island, and ideally someone who is meaningful to you personally. That doesn't mean you have to be related to them." Watras smiled at Sarah, who bragged to anyone who would listen that she was a direct descendant of Alexander Hamilton. "But that you see yourself in them in some way. Tell us why the rest of Staten Island should appreciate them too. Any other questions?"

"What's contemporary?" asked Jason.

Watras sighed to say both that he'd known the question was coming and that it was too annoying that we didn't know to have told us in the first place.

"*Contemporary* refers to the now. So, no Alyssa Milano. No rappers."

"What about Randy 'Macho Man' Savage?" asked Rebekkah. "He lived on Staten Island."

"Who?"

"The wrestler. He died in 2011. Does that count as not contemporary?"

Watras pressed the pads of his index fingers to the bridge of his neck and muttered something to himself. "No, Rebekkah. No Randy Savage. No Sammy the Bull either."

"Who's Sammy the Bull?" asked Rhyan.

"You betta be cay-ful askin' questions." A few kids laughed

at Anthony's impression of a thick Italian American accent. "Sammy da Bull, he don't like peoples askin' no questions they's don't need da answahs to."

"That's enough, De Niro. My point is, no one from this century. They can be from politics, arts, culture, science, even sports." Watras eyed Rebekkah. "But go back. Do some research and learn some history."

Watras answered a few more questions with the same tone of mild irritation until the bell rang, and he shooed the class off to "go bother some other teachers for a while."

"Ugh," I said the moment I reached TJ's desk, but TJ pointed their eyes over at Watras to say *let's get outside first.*

Once we were in the din of the hallway, TJ shouted, "WORST."

"PROJECT." That was me.

"EVER!" We shouted it together.

To be fair, this was not the first time that TJ and I had called an assignment the worst project ever. It wasn't even the first time that year. But just about any history project was automatically worthy of consideration for the title, and this one sounded especially dreadful. Even the fact that it was a pair project and we'd get to work on it together didn't make it much better.

"I'm not doing a project on a straight white man," said TJ.

"Me either."

History was full of straight white men and even most of the people who weren't straight pretended they were. So we were supposed to find someone cool from history *and* they were supposed to be important to Staten Island?

It wasn't just the worst project ever—it was the most impossible project ever.

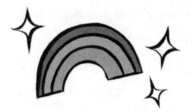

CHAPTER FOUR

The more I thought about it, the more I wanted our project to be about someone queer. I did a little googling on queer Staten Islanders, but not much came up. One article said that there were almost no statues of LGBTQIAP+ icons in New York City, much less Staten Island. Another said that fewer than ten of more than one hundred fifty statues of historical people around the city were women, and I was willing to bet that the remaining one hundred forty plus were all men. I was glad I would be seeing Jess after school on Tuesday. If she didn't have any ideas, Val certainly would. Val had been born on Staten Island, and they were always talking about queer history.

I left my shoes at the door and found Jess in the living room, feeding Evie. She was stretched out in her cozy recliner with a thick purple blanket draped over her and Evie, so that the top of Evie's head barely peeked out from under it and

Jess's breasts were covered. Jess had taught me to say *breast* the first time she fed Evie when I was around. We practiced saying it together, and then she gave me homework to say it at home in front of a mirror until I could say it without hesitating, whispering, or giggling, the same way I'd say *arm* or *knee*. Breast.

"Hey, Sam."

"Hey, Jess. Iced tea?"

"Yes, please."

Jess always wanted iced tea while she was nursing, but I hadn't ever seen her remember to get some before she started. I pulled two mason jars out of a cabinet, popped three ice cubes into one, and filled them both from the pitcher of home-brewed tea in the fridge.

"Does it really count as iced tea if you don't put any ice in it?" Jess asked when I gave her the glass with ice. I don't like my drinks to be too cold.

"Does it really count as a joke if you've said it ten times before?" I replied.

"Oooh! Good one! You've got some fire in you today."

"I do what I can." I shrugged nonchalantly, but *fire* was the highest compliment she gave.

Jess took another sip and then shifted Evie over to the other breast.

"So, how's the state-funded brainwashing going?" Jess asked.

"School? We have to do this report on a historical figure."

"Sounds like fun."

"Sounds like you don't understand fun very well," I told her.

"Sounds like your sarcast-o-meter needs new batteries."

I told Jess about the group project Watras had assigned and the research I had done.

"History is littered with queer icons," Jess said. "Sylvia Rivera. Bayard Rustin. Even Alexander the Great is suspected to have been intimate with men, though he wasn't working with our modern notions of gay and straight."

"Yeah, but Alexander the Great isn't from Staten Island, is he?"

"Fair point," said Jess. "Let's check in with Val later, and see what they think."

Jess finished feeding Evie and settled her into her bouncer seat. Then we went through Jess's closet to bag up the pants she wore when she was pregnant and her stomach stretched out wide.

When Val got home, they gave a kiss to Jess, a hug to me, and then lifted Evie out of her bouncer seat to curl up on the couch with her in their lap. As they bounced

Evie up and down, they said "a-ma-ma-ma-ma-ma" and "a-da-da-da-da-da." Sometimes she would make a sound of her own, like "pbbbbbtttbbbhhh" or "ehhhh," and Val would copy it back at her.

After a few minutes, Val lifted their head, as if remembering that the rest of the world was still here.

"What's up, Sam!" they asked.

I told them about the statue assignment and how TJ and I didn't want to do a project about someone who wasn't queer.

"I see the conundrum," said Val. "There are some subconscious assumptions on the part of your teacher that hypothetically overlaying ourselves onto the past works equivalently for all parties."

"Okay, Professor Cutepants, dial it down." Jess patted Val's knee. "In commonspeak for the rest of us, please."

Val was a graduate student and teaching assistant at The New School in Manhattan, and sometimes it showed.

"Have you ever heard that time travel is for white men?" Val asked.

"No," I said.

Val explained. "Basically, if a cishet, abled-bodied white guy goes back in time, he's still a cishet, abled-bodied white guy. He might not blend in. He might not even speak the language, but . . ."

"All the times are good times for white guys," Jess completed the thought.

"Exactly." Val continued. "But if one of us went back in time, we could be in trouble. There are plenty of times and places in America when I wouldn't be welcome because I'm Latinx."

"Plus, the queer thing," Jess said. "I mean, I *might* be okay, being femme and all, but plenty of places could be bad for a nonbinary gentlequeer like Val." *Gentlequeer* was a gender-free way of saying *gentleman.*

"Exactly," said Val. "And it's not like things were great for women in most times, femme or not."

"But what does this have to do with my project?" I asked.

"For the white boys in your class, it's going to be relatively simple to find someone from Staten Island's history to connect with. But for the white girls and queer folk, especially the trans and nonbinary folk, and for all the people of color, there are additional barriers to success. They either limit themselves to the few people who managed to break through in their time or they have to add an extra layer of translation to their process."

"A what now?" I said.

"Val." Jess's voice went syrupy sweet. "Are you saying that this project's going to be easier for white boys because there are so many white boys in the history books to choose from?"

"Well, yeah."

"I knew *that*," I said.

Val ignored me. Once they were in academic mode, they tended to go on. "And while you can choose to focus on a DSCWM, it's more work to connect." *DSCWM* was Val's acronym for *Dead Straight Cisgender White Man*. They pronounced it *disk-wum*.

"I don't *want* to do a report about a DSCWM!" I folded my arms across my chest. "And I don't want to theorize about what it means that my teacher gave us this assignment! I just wish there were someone queer from the past I could connect with."

"What about Oscar Wilde?" Val suggested. "Your senses of humor are a solid match."

"Did he live in New York City?" My words felt a little sharper than I meant them, but if Val noticed, they didn't say anything.

Instead, they shook their head and said, "England."

"Darling, do you think I couldn't have come up with Oscar?" Jess tossed her head, and her bobbed hair followed. "I mean, really now!"

"Sorry, love, that one's on me. So, they've got to be a Knickerbocker."

"They have to play for the Knicks?" I asked.

"No—a Knickerbocker is a New Yawkah!" Val said as

if they were hitting a taxi on the hood while sauntering through a crosswalk.

"It's not just New York in general," I reminded Val. "They need to have a connection to Staten Island."

Val sat back in their chair, crossed one leg over the other knee, and stroked the fine hairs along their upper jawline. They stared at the ceiling, their tongue rubbing along the bottom of their top teeth as they thought. Then they sat up with a start. "I've got it. I've got it!" They typed something into their phone and nodded at themself with approval. "Yes, yes, I've really got it!"

"Great!" said Jess. "Now give it to the rest of us!"

"Of course! So, the person I'm thinking of isn't trans or nonbinary, so far as we know, but she lived her entire life on Staten Island, and she had a long-term woman partner."

"*She* is good. Partner is good," I said. "Who is it?"

"Have you ever heard of Alice Austen?"

"Like the ferry?" asked Jess.

"Exactly like the ferry!"

The ferry boats to Manhattan each had a name, and you could see it in huge letters when you boarded. The only one I remembered was the *John F. Kennedy*, because of the time TJ's grandma came to visit; we all took the ferry, and she told us about how his assassination changed her childhood.

"Austen was a local photographer." Val handed their phone to Jess, who scrolled up and down with wide eyes of delight.

"Lemme see!" I demanded, and Jess gave me Val's phone, the screen showing a black-and-white picture of three white men at the beach in old-fashioned bathing suits, one man with his hand on another's head, and all three of them casually smiling at the camera. Another photo showed a young adult Alice and five friends gathered on a tennis court with tennis racquets, one of them pretending to play it like a banjo.

I scrolled past an image of two grumpy little kids sitting back-to-back on a cart, and another with two more kids selling newspapers as they squinted in the sunshine. Two women with ballooning pants held the handlebars of their bicycles. There was a picture of an old, beautiful house and one of a cluttered living room filled with ornate metal tables, shelves full of vases, giant-fronded ferns, a massive throne-like chair, and more. They were intriguing photographs. The people in them felt real. It was like I was seeing the world through Alice's eyes, even when she was in the photo herself.

And then I saw the picture that really sealed the deal: three people in suits, two standing in the grass in front of some vines, and one sitting in the middle. The caption said that Alice was on the left, and the two people were her friends, Julia Martin and Julia Bredt. They looked happy as could be, in their vests and fancy hats, cigarettes in two of their hands, the third with her hands in her pin-striped pants pockets.

Alice definitely looked queer in that picture. Maybe all three of them were queer. Watras had asked us to find someone to connect with, and I had done it—with Val's help.

"Val! You're amazing!" I yelled before giving them back their phone.

"I do what I can," Val said calmly, but it was clear they were proud to have come up with a winner. "Here's to Alice Austen becoming a statue I get to walk by on the way to the ferry!"

"I'll belly bump to that!" I said, and Jess waved me over to her seat on the couch where we pressed our stomachs together.

"Belly power!" we yelled.

"And get this," said Val, scrolling through the page. "Her partner's name was Gertrude Tate!"

"You have got to be kidding me!" Jess tossed her head back in laughter.

"What's so funny?" I asked.

"Ever heard of Gertrude Stein?"

I shook my head.

"She was a famous lesbian poet, and she had a long-term partner, Alice B. Toklas."

"So this was another Gertrude and Alice," Jess said.

"Or perhaps this was Alice and Gertrude," Val replied.

Gertrude and Alice. Alice and Gertrude. No matter how you said it, Alice Austen was a *fabulous* idea for our project.

"I know who we're going to do our report on!" I told TJ the next morning as we walked to the stop for the city bus we took to school.

They shook their head. "Sometimes it couldn't be more obvious that you're an only child."

"What do you mean?"

"You don't know the first thing about getting buy-in."

"What?"

"Buy-in. In my house, when I have an idea, I can't just go around saying, *I have an idea*. That's asking for someone to fight me on why my idea sucks. But"—TJ raised a finger to accentuate the turn—"if I start hinting at an idea and they think they came up with it first, all I have to do is fight it enough that they think they won."

"Okay then, what about this? I found an amazing person who I'm going to do my project on, and if you don't like her, you can do a project with someone else."

"My mom calls that *My Way or the Highway*. Are you saying you don't want to work with me?"

"Not at all!" I said.

"*Then* why don't you just tell me who it is and I'll tell you what I think?"

"Oh. Right." I paused for a dramatic reveal. "Alice Austen."

TJ looked at me blankly. "More data needed."

"She was a photographer from the early nineteen hundreds, when cameras were still pretty new."

"Photographer? That's cool. Keep going."

"Val told me about her. She was a lesbian, and she lived on Staten Island her whole life. There's even a ferry named after her."

"Which is clearly a sign of local significance," noted TJ with a whiff of condescension in their voice.

"Don't mock me."

"I wasn't mocking you. I was mocking Watras. Tell me more about this Alice Austen."

I told TJ what I had learned with Jess and Val, including about Gertrude Tate and that Alice had taken pictures in both dresses and suits. Once TJ heard that fashion was involved, their voice got excited, and when we reached the bus stop, they pulled out their tablet. Moments later, they were scrolling through black-and-white photographs, saying,

"That hat!" and "That dress!" and "Those bow ties!" They also pointed out that there was an Alice Austen museum on Staten Island, so our next step was clear. By the time the bus had arrived, they were convinced.

"Luckily, you're not my sibling, so I have no problem telling you that you are absolutely right," said TJ with a sure look. "Alice here is perfect for our project, and perfect for Staten Island's newest statue."

CHAPTER FIVE

I loved having two best friends, especially when all three of us could do something together, like when Jess agreed to drive TJ and me to the Alice Austen House Museum that Saturday. Evie came along too.

Evie's car seat was in the back, so I sat up front with Jess while TJ sat behind me. The latest Miss Chris song came on the radio, and the three of us sang along together on the short drive over. Jess didn't know the verses as well as TJ and I did, but she knew the chorus and she could hit the high notes.

The Alice Austen House Museum wasn't a museum like the big ones in Manhattan with armor and dinosaur bones. Instead, it was the house that Alice had lived in for most of her life, from the time she was little until she lost her money and had to move. The house was named Clear Comfort.

After her death, people convinced the city to buy it and turn it into a museum.

Jess parked on the last (or first, depending on how you looked at it) block of Hylan Boulevard. TJ and I ran down to take in the view, just a few large stones from the water that flowed from New York Harbor to the Atlantic Ocean. The southwest tip of Brooklyn lay directly across from us, with the Verrazzano-Narrows Bridge on our right. The clump of gray points and rectangles that made up downtown Manhattan popped out of the water on our left, and off in the far left presided the little green spot that was the Statue of Liberty. Long barges dotted the bay, the distance masking their massive size.

"My great-grandpa was a longshoreman, you know," said TJ, picking up a pebble and tossing it into the water with a splash.

"What's a longshoreman?" I asked.

"A dock worker. He was one of the guys who would take the stuff off the boat and put it on trucks or wagons, or whatever they used back then."

"Cool." I picked up a small, jagged rock and plopped it into the water. The ripples expanded out to meet the rings from TJ's pebble.

"Do you think Alice ever saw one of the boats he unloaded going by?"

"I don't think so," TJ said. "When did she die?"

"In 1952. But she and Gertrude went bankrupt and got kicked out of here in 1945."

"And when did World War II end?"

"The 1950s or something, I think."

"1945!" called Jess, who walked toward us, adjusting Evie's carrier straps. "I thought you were good with numbers."

"I was close!" I called back. "Besides, that's history, not math."

"No, then," said TJ. "He wasn't old enough to enter the army during World War II, and Grandma said he complained about it until the day he died. But maybe Alice saw my great-great-grandpa sailing in from Italy. His name was Giuseppe Pulcinella." They said it with a bouncing cadence, so it sounded like *Juh-SAY-pey PULCH-ih-NELL-eh*. "Don't ask me to spell it. He immigrated in 1915, when he was about our age."

TJ's grandma on their mom's side was a genealogist, and every July, TJ and their siblings spent a month with her in North Carolina. They complained about the misery of going every year, but they always came back with amazing family stories and an extra glow in their cheeks that hinted at barbecue and peaches.

I did the math. Alice was almost fifty when Giuseppe had entered the country. She could have been sitting on the porch, having tea with Gertrude, when his ship went by. He might have been one of the people waving at the shores of his new home. Alice might have waved back, or even taken a photo of his ship coming in.

And back when she was a kid, she could have been playing in the same yard, watching the pieces of Lady Liberty on their way in from France. The large pieces of copper were still the color of a new penny then and probably shone brightly as they passed.

"So, you two ready to go in?" Jess asked.

TJ and I turned around and there it was—Clear Comfort. The black-and-white photos Alice had taken of it came to colorful life, with its three gabled windows that stuck out from the steeply sloped roof like cubes with triangular hats. There were even wicker rocking chairs on the long porch. I could practically see Alice and Gertrude sharing afternoon tea with their friends, laughing about their latest adventures.

The moment we walked inside, we were greeted by an older white couple behind a cash register wearing matching ALICE AUSTEN HOUSE MUSEUM baseball caps and T-shirts. The woman appeared eager to have patrons, but the man looked like he would have been just as happy to have read his paper in peace. Jess paid the woman for three admissions.

"So I guess you plan to leave the little one outside?" the man said, revealing a grin that said that as long as he was going to be disturbed, he might as well enjoy himself.

"Martin!" the woman admonished the man. "Don't mind him. He loves children."

"For breakfast, lunch, and dinner!" said Martin, before ducking behind his newspaper away from the woman's glare. It was clear he was one of those guys that liked to pretend he was a lot grumpier than he actually was.

"In any event, my name's Lillian, and this is my husband, Martin. Here are your tickets, and of course, there's no charge for the baby. If you have any questions about the museum, we would be happy to help you. Alice Austen was an amazing figure, you know."

"She sure was," said Jess, who continued to chat with Lillian while Martin went back to reading. TJ and I headed into the museum's first room, with its old-fashioned wallpaper and roped-off chairs. There was a pair of glass displays of items from the Clear Comfort home, including a heavy metal bell, a serving tray, and strips of old wallpaper—Alice's family's things, but not really Alice. Even the photos were of Alice's relatives, mostly taken before Alice was born. One of the photo notes said that Alice lived as the only child at Clear Comfort, with her mom, grandparents, and three aunts and uncles.

"Look," I said. "She was an only kid too."

"Lucky," said TJ. "C'mon, let's go find some photos Alice took herself."

Jess peered into a cabinet filled with fine china and crystal the family had collected while we explored the rest of the house-sized museum and found the room dedicated to her photography, including a display in the center of the room for her beloved camera.

The room felt totally different from the living room, and not just because it was less cluttered. It felt like Alice, from the display of downtown Manhattan street shots showing kids and horse-drawn carriages filling cobblestone streets to the projection that covered one wall with a revolving slide show. The series went through beach shots, beautiful old houses, and groups of friends hanging out in boats and on rocks.

We were really in Alice's home, watching pictures Alice had taken flip across the wall. It was so real it started to feel unreal again, like when you're so happy that you can't believe what's happening is real.

Then TJ's face broke into a grin, the one that says they've figured something out.

"That's the one," they said, their eyes locked in front of them.

"Okay." I waited for more, but TJ just beamed. "The one what?"

They gestured at a row of eleven small photos hung across the length of one wall. "The design for the statue."

"Oh," I said. "Which one?" They were the queerest photos in the room, including an image of Alice and two other women sharing a bed, as well as two women smoking each others' cigarettes. There was even the picture of Alice and her friends smiling in suits.

"The big one."

"The big one?"

"The big one."

And then I saw it—behind the row of framed photos was a much bigger image on the wall itself. Four larger-than-life women stood outdoors facing each other in two pairs, looking deeply into each other's eyes, with their hands around each other's waists, just above where their long skirts puffed out. They looked delighted to be together, and if anyone had ever told them women shouldn't look at each other like that, they had clearly decided to ignore the advice. A plaque identified Alice as the woman on the left, embracing her friend Trude Eccleston. The other pair was Julia Marsh and Sue Ripley. The location was the Clear Comfort lawn. It was the same place we had been throwing rocks a few minutes earlier.

The photograph was called *The Darned Club*, and the plaque said that's what people on Staten Island called Alice and her friends. They looked carefree. Happy to be themselves. Even better, they looked very, very queer.

"Oh! Yes! That is definitely the one!" I raced through the

museum, looking for Jess and avoiding Martin's glare, yelling, "We found it! We found it!"

"What did you find?" asked Jess, followed by a mouthed *sorry* toward Martin. She was still in the first room. I led her by the hand to the enlarged photo that TJ was still taking in.

"This!" I said. "This is what we want the statue to look like."

"Wow," said Jess, taking in the double embrace. "This is amazing. I knew Alice had a woman partner, but this is . . . well . . . it's amazing!"

"I know!" said TJ. "Just look at those fabric folds. Those collars. That bustle!"

"Also the queer love. And what a name they earned for themselves, *The Darned Club*. When was this taken?" Jess looked over at the plaque. "1891! Wow!"

The Statue of Liberty had been only five years old then, just to the left of the photo.

If our statue was chosen, the women would face each other from across the bay.

CHAPTER SIX

Watras insisted that we needed to use at least one physical book as research for our project. So even though we had already read about her online, and even gone to her home and found the perfect queer image for our statue, TJ and I had to find a book about Alice Austen.

On Sunday morning, before Nacious's walk, I checked the New York Public Library website and found a book called *Alice's World* by Ann Novotny.

"There's a copy available in Tottenville," I told TJ, who was sprawled out on my bed.

"Why in heck is it in *Tottenville*? Tottenville's all the way on the other side of the island. If Alice Austen went to the library, she would have gone to the St. George branch."

"There's a copy there too."

"Then why don't we get that one?" TJ threw up their hands in an exaggerated act of indignation.

"Because it's in the reference section. That means we have to look at it there." You weren't allowed to take books out of the reference section, not even if you needed them for a report. I knew for sure because I'd asked once.

"You're so antisocial," TJ chided.

"I'm an introvert."

"I'm pretty sure libraries are like parties for introverts."

"Books *are* better than people."

"Hey! I'm a people!" TJ wrinkled their face in mock offense.

"Okay, books are better than *most* people. But I was thinking it would be better to have it for when you sketch our statue proposal."

"Oh, *I'm* sketching it?"

"Do you really want me to sketch it?"

TJ looked at me, shaking their head tightly. "No. You'll mess up the dress lines. But that means you have to type the essay."

"Deal."

I requested the copy of the book, and we watched videos online of people setting up obstacle courses in their backyards until it was time to walk Nacious.

The following Saturday morning, I got a text that *Alice's World* had arrived at the St. George branch. Now I just had to get there. I wasn't allowed to cross more than one street from my home alone, and I was pretty sure the only reason I was allowed that far was so my mom could send me to the deli. I was only allowed to walk to the bus stop, which is across the street from the library, because TJ walked with me. If TJ was out sick, Mom drove me to school. But if I was out sick, TJ was allowed to go to school alone. They called it one of the advantages of being the middle child in a house full of kids. They could probably take the train to Tottenville alone if they wanted.

Mom was attending a weekend-long conference online, and TJ's family was in South Jersey, at a family reunion on their dad's side. Sure, I could have waited until Monday to pick it up, but there was a book filled with pictures Alice had taken just waiting for me. I wanted to see it right away, so I pulled out my phone.

SamSaysSo: wanna go to the library?

SamSaysSo: Alice's book came in

JessSinger: Val and I have plans for the day

SamSaysSo: I thought you said you weren't going anywhere

JessSinger: those are exactly our plans. Val isn't teaching this weekend and they promised not to do any work today

SamSaysSo: it'll only take half an hour. is Val even up yet?

JessSinger: no

SamSaysSo: please? I'll watch Evie for you later

JessSinger: you'd do that anyway

SamSaysSo: but I'll get Mom to let me watch her up here so you can, you know . . . have some alone time

JessSinger: I'm still in my pjs

SamSaysSo: so am I!

SamSaysSo: pretty please

SamSaysSo: the pictures of queers are calling me

SamSaysSo: they're calling me, Jess!

I sent an animated gif of a pug stretched up on their hind legs, feebly attempting to reach a tennis ball that had rolled to the back of the couch cushion.

JessSinger: ok fine

JessSinger: meet me in the lobby in 30 min

SamSaysSo: YAAAaaAAAaaAAYYYYYY!!!!!!!

SamSaysSo: thank you thank you thank you!

SamSaysSo: it'll be super fast

JessSinger: it had better be

I was downstairs in half an hour, sitting on the low stone walls that bordered the walkway from the street to the front door of our building. Twenty-eight minutes actually. I couldn't blame Jess for not being there during those two minutes, but I could blame her for not being there for the eighteen more it took her to show up. Eighteen minutes that I had to wait to take the same walk I took to the bus with TJ almost every day. I could have made the trip there and back in that time.

Okay, so the fact that I had to wait was really Mom's fault, because if she was a normal mom, I would have just been able to go. And if I'd been a different kind of kid, I would have simply gone and later told my mom that Jess went with me. But I didn't think I could keep up a lie like that, and I didn't want to be the kind of kid who could. So it wasn't all

Jess's fault, and what I said when she finally appeared wasn't exactly fair, but she was late, and best friends weren't supposed to keep each other waiting if they could help it.

"What took you so long?" I asked.

"Excuse me?" Jess drew her chin back and looked down at me in a most un-best-friend-like way. "I can turn around and head right back upstairs, young queer."

I hated when she called me young. It was bad enough that it was true without her reminding me that she thought about it sometimes.

"Sorry."

"Whatever." Jess started walking toward the library. I followed her. We were quiet for the first block, and by the time Jess spoke again, her voice was back to normal.

"So I get that you're excited for this book, but why aren't you going with TJ? It's their project too."

"They're away for the weekend."

"And it couldn't wait until Monday?"

"Fifty-three more hours?! This is queer culture, Jess, and you *know* how important that is to people like us."

"Fifty-three hours, eh?"

"Two whole days, plus another five hours until school would be over."

Jess shook her head, but she chuckled and said something to herself about the *innocent impatience of youth.* Then she started telling me about the blueberry pancakes she was going to make when she got back home. When we reached the library, she took a seat on a wide set of steps across the street, leaning back with her arms stretched behind her. Her hair shone in the sunshine as she looked up at the blue sky peppered with clouds.

Inside, there was no line at the desk, and less than a minute later I was holding *Alice's World*. It was large and heavy and covered in a layer of plastic. A black-and-white photo showed eight people gathered around a table for tea. The men wore suits, and a standing woman had a dress tailored to her waist with big buttons and a wide collar. The intricately floral wallpaper peeked out between photographs in large frames. Some of the people looked serious, and some were having a good time, but no one else seemed to notice the two young men up front. One of them was lying on the floor, eyes looking up as if he was dreaming or something, or maybe just drunk. And his legs were up against another guy, who had his hand on his forehead like he'd just remembered he was supposed to text his mom an hour ago. His arm draped over the lying boy's legs, one of which had a saucer balanced on it.

Between the title and the photo were the words *The Life and Photography of an American Original: Alice Austen, 1866–1952, by Ann Novotny*. 1952 was closer to now than it was to

1866, but not by much. I checked out the book and brought it outside to where Jess was waiting. I showed it to her proudly.

"Some photo!" she said.

I wanted to look through it immediately, or at least belly bump to celebrate, but Jess had already started walking toward the corner. The trip here had been pleasant, but it was clear she was ready to get back home. I stuffed the book in my backpack and managed to get the zipper over the corners.

"Thank you, Jess!" I ran up to her and hugged her tight, my arms stretched around her waist.

"You're welcome," Jess said matter-of-factly.

"And I promise to watch Evie all afternoon."

"Oh, you will." Jess nodded for emphasis. "I'll bring her up after her nap."

"And she can stay as long as you want."

"I know."

When I got home, I flipped through the pictures. Some of them were familiar from our trip to Clear Comfort, like *The Darned Club*, and a few I'd seen online, like the grumpy kids in the cart, but others were new to me, or at least I hadn't noticed them at the museum. More pictures of her family, Staten Island, and downtown Manhattan.

There were photos of Alice's friend Daisy Elliott demonstrating how to ride a bicycle. The caption said they had to use sticks to keep the bike upright so that Alice could take the photos. Cameras back then had long exposures so people had to stay very still in order for the picture not to blur. There was even a picture of Alice standing next to her pug and I thought about how funny it would be if it were Nacious's great-great-great-great-great-great-grandmother or something.

There were lots of pictures with Alice's friends too: playing tennis, at the beach, in the water, gathered around a table, on the porch. Anywhere you could expect friends to be, Alice was there with them.

And then there was Gertrude Tate, Alice's long-term partner. Pictures showed them together, whether touring Europe or in the garden at Clear Comfort. In one photo near the end of the book, Alice was seated on the left, with Gertrude proudly standing next to her, Gertrude's arm leaning on Alice's chair. Alice's hair was peppery gray by then and Gertrude's looked pure white, though it was hard to know for sure in the black-and-white picture. A camera sat at Alice's side, because she had just been taking pictures herself. They both looked confident about how they'd lived their lives.

Seeing Alice with her friends and partner was almost like hanging out with them. These photos were like the pictures I take with TJ and Jess, just in black and white. And over a hundred years old.

CHAPTER SEVEN

The next morning, I put *Alice's World* in my backpack and headed downstairs to meet TJ. On the way to the bus stop, they talked about their weekend with their cousins. It was great, because it meant I could nod and say "yeah" occasionally without having to hold up the conversation myself.

Alice's World was too much on my mind to think about anything else, but I couldn't show it to them just yet. I hadn't texted them that it had arrived because I wanted to surprise them, but if I brought it up now, TJ might insist on stopping right where we were and looking at the book until we missed the bus and officially became late for school. Not that I would blame them, and normally, I wouldn't mind, except that I had a first-period quiz in math.

A mostly empty bus pulled up a few minutes later, and we slid into a two-seater. I took the window spot, backpack in my lap, and TJ swung in next to me as the bus pulled away from the curb. In the other direction, a packed bus passed by, ready to drop its passengers off at the ferry.

"Wanna see what I got this weekend?"

"Is it the reason your bag's so pointy?"

"Yep," I said as I tugged the zipper around a book corner.

"Is that what I think it is?"

"Probably, unless you think it's something really weird." I handed over *Alice's World*. TJ ran their fingers across the cover, just as I had done last night. The plastic gave it an inviting shine.

"When did you get it?"

"Saturday morning."

"Sam! You've had this book all weekend, and you're just telling me about it now?"

"Imagine if I told you when you were in Jersey that I was at home, looking through it."

TJ tipped their head to the side for a moment and then nodded. "Fair. But it's mine to take home tonight."

"Of course. And in the meantime, we can store it in one of our lockers for the day."

"Are you kidding me? I'm not letting this baby out of my sight." They opened it and flipped through the early pages, past the pictures of Alice's older relatives and her garden self-portrait.

Other kids were loading onto the bus at each stop, and now there were nearly as many kids standing as sitting, backpacks pressed against each other and the whoosh of the bus's engine was drowned out by a growing conversational hum and intermittent shrieks of joy, anger, and embarrassment. The few adults on the bus held their bags and looked like they hoped we would reach the school soon.

TJ paused on the two-page spread of beach photos. The wide shot of the water looked like Midland Beach today, with crowds of people standing, bobbing, and swimming. But in the close-ups, you could tell that the photos were old because their beachwear reached from their necks to their knees.

"Beachwear with a collar. Now that's dedication to fashion." TJ pointed out the woman wearing what looked like a button-down, collared sleeveless dress. "And look at all those bold stripes. I wish we knew what colors they were. Maybe bright white and navy blue."

TJ was still deep in the book when the tree-lined winding road reached a red light at a corner with a deli and a laundromat. The bus stop, and our school, were on the other side of the street. They kept turning the pages as the bus crossed the street, and even as students poured out. I was already waiting on the sidewalk when TJ closed the book and joined the last few kids filing off the bus.

I noticed TJ sneak a peek at the pictures in the book

between classes when they could, but it wasn't until l··· -ˡ that they really got to pore over the photos again.

The school cafeteria was brightly lit with a wall of n grated windows that left a diamond pattern on the floor in the darker corners of the room. The walls were filled with posters about nutrition and signs about what can be recycled and composted and where to put empty trays. Above the kitchen itself was a giant banner that reminded students, BITES AND BYTES DON'T MATCH! NO ELECTRONICS IN THE CAFETERIA.

Middle school lunch is terrible. I know it, you know it, and TJ's parents, the chef and the nutritionist, know it. And it's not just that it tastes bad. When you compare it to what kids get served in other countries, or even what they get served in high school, it's clear that whoever's making middle school lunches is not prioritizing nutrition *or* health. Plus, TJ had a lot of allergies and had to be careful what they ate. They couldn't have any wheat or soy, and you might be surprised at the kinds of things that have bits of wheat and soy in them. That's why we always brought our lunches from home. My favorite was what I called picnic lunch: crackers, cheese, olives, sunflower seeds, carrot sticks, and whatever fruit Mom had around. Sometimes there was even a piece or two of chocolate for dessert.

TJ quickly finished the gourmet grain-and-veggie bowl their dad had made and wiped down their part of the table while I picked at my meal. Their reactions to the fashions and candid queer shots were at least as entertaining as the photos themselves.

"O! M! G!" TJ cried for the hundredth time. "Can you even believe those buttons? That hat? Those cuffs? That hemline?" And "Who knew how hot everyone was a hundred years ago! Just look at that boy. At least, I think he's a boy."

But then TJ did something I hadn't thought to do. They started reading the text on some of the pages. A real detective type.

"Sam."

"Yeah?"

"Sam."

"Ye-ah?"

"SAM!"

"WHAT?"

TJ blinked dramatically at the page. Their mouth was open, but no more words were coming out. I wasn't sure they were even breathing.

"Are you okay?"

TJ nodded slowly. "She was there," they said in a whisper.

"Who?"

"She was *there*," TJ repeated.

"Are you aware that you sound like the creepy kid in a horror movie?"

"Look!" TJ slid over the book and pointed at a line halfway down the page that said that Alice and Gertrude had moved to 141 St. Mark's Place, Apartment 5-C in 1945. As in ONE-*forty-onnnnne, ST! MARK'S! PLACE! a-PART-ment, FIIIIVE CEEEEE.* As in . . .

"That's where I live!"

Alice Austen had lived in my apartment. Or I was living in Alice Austen's apartment. Either way, I couldn't wait to get home and be in my room, looking out my window, knowing that Alice once had the same view.

"I can't believe it! A real live queer lived in my apartment, more than seventy years ago." Then I paused. "Oh wait, do you still want to do this project?"

"Are you kidding me? We've worked on it for hours. We went to Clear Comfort together. Why in the world would you think I would want to ditch now?"

I shrugged. "I just don't want to be selfish."

"Selfish?"

"I mean, Alice Austen was my idea, and now she lived in my building."

"What about the outfits they wore? And I'm queer and from Staten Island too, you know. This project is at least as much about me as it is about you. Besides, she lived in my best friend's apartment. What could be cooler than that? Stop trying to figure out what I need."

"But what if I don't know what you need?"

"Um, Sam, there's this funny little trick called . . . asking."

"Oh. Right."

"Watch this: Sam, can I come over to your house after school?"

"Of course. I'll text my mom so she knows you're coming."

"Text Jess too. Because we are going to go over and *ask* her if she knows anything about who used to live there."

"But I've lived there longer than Jess has. I was even born there. Or, well, I was born at the hospital, but you know what I mean. In fact, my parents were living there for a year already, so I was living there before I was born."

"And how many of your neighbors do you know?"

"Well, there's Jess and Val and Evie, and Ms. Hansen and Nacious downstairs, and the Taylors across the hall."

"Out of forty apartments, you can name three?"

"And my apartment. That's ten percent."

"Those aren't exactly social butterfly numbers."

"Whatever. Kids aren't supposed to talk to strangers."

TJ gave me a side-eye look, which was fair. I wasn't sure whether people who lived in your building were officially strangers, and besides, TJ had a point. Jess always said hi to people when she saw them in the hall or the elevator, and she usually knew their names.

"Okay, fine," I said. "We'll go see Jess after school."

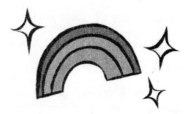

CHAPTER EIGHT

TJ carried the book home from the bus stop, which was good because it was uphill and TJ was taller and stronger than me. We made our way between high school students milling around and crowding the sidewalk, laughing and yelling and complaining about everything from teachers and parents to the school-to-prison pipeline.

141 St. Mark's Place faced the back of Curtis High School. When I was little, I was excited that when I got older, I would be able to wake up ten minutes before school started and still be on time. If my first class was in the right part of the building, I could even use a ladder to climb in the window and not have to go all the way down the block to the main entrance. And if I left an important project at home, I would be able to go back and get it in minutes. But now that I was actually in seventh grade, the idea of regular high school was kind

of terrifying. New York City had a lot of specialty schools, but if I didn't get in to any of them, I thought I might talk to Mom about homeschooling. I didn't know if she'd go for it, but every day on the way home from the bus, TJ and I had to avoid collisions with high school boys who pushed each other around, and I didn't want to have to do that all day long.

I pressed the button for the fifth floor out of habit, and we were already at the third when I reached and pressed four as well. Even when I visited Jess after school, I usually dropped my things off at home first and took the stairs down. But that day we were in a rush, and all too often when TJ came over, they would notice some new decor piece that Mom had put up and would get into a long discussion about how she had crafted it.

Jess invited us to join her in the living room, where a plate of oatmeal cookies sat on the coffee table. Evie was chewing on her toes in her baby seat on the floor. She was too young for cookies.

"Care for one?" She offered the plate toward TJ. "They're still warm."

"I can't eat wheat."

"They're gluten-free," Jess said.

"And those are chocolate chips, not raisins," I added.

TJ looked at Jess for confirmation, who nodded with a proud smile.

"Jess would never do us wrong by putting raisins in a cookie." I grabbed one for myself.

"No soy in them, right?" TJ asked.

"None. I would have one right now, except that I've already eaten a half dozen since they came out of the oven and my teeth are just about caked in chocolate." She put the plate on the coffee table.

"These are delicious!" said TJ.

"Everything Jess bakes is delicious." Then I took a bite myself. "Oh wow! These *are* delicious." Jess was right. They were still warm, and that meant the chocolate was especially gooey and the oats tasted especially toasty.

"So, what did you want to tell me about?" Jess asked. "You said it was incredible, Sam, so I'm ready to be impressed."

"Alice Austen lived here!" I blurted.

"Yeah, I know. We all went to Clear Comfort together. I drove you there."

"No, not here as in Staten Island. Here as in *this building*. 141 St. Mark's Place! In 5-C! THAT'S MY APARTMENT!"

"That is impressive." Jess sounded less excited than I'd expected. Maybe it was different because Alice lived in my apartment, not hers, but Jess sounded amused where she should be enthused. That was even Jess's line. I hated to use it against her, but it was true.

"But wait," said Jess. "She lived at Clear Comfort."

"She did for most of her life. But then she lost all her money and she and Gertrude ended up moving here for a couple of years. Can you even believe it? There was someone queer living in this building back in 1945."

"At least one!" said Jess. "I wonder if Leslie knew them. She's lived here longer than anyone else."

"Leslie?" I took a second cookie and so did TJ.

"You know, the lesbian on the first floor? With the pug?"

"Do you mean Ms. Hansen?" TJ said.

"In 1-C."

"Wait, are you saying Ms. Hansen is a lesbian?" My mouth hung open a bit, and I'll bet there were still bits of cookie on my lips. Ms. Hansen was kind of cool, but I'd never thought about whether she was queer.

"She might be bisexual, but yeah, I'm pretty sure she's part of the family."

"How do you know?"

"Well, I wasn't sure at first," said Jess, "so I made a couple of references, and she picked up on every one of them. She's one of us. You don't think all queer people are young, do you?"

"No, no. Of course not." Dang it. That was exactly what I'd done.

"No stereotyping now. Besides, if Alice Austen was alive today, she'd be way older than Leslie."

"If Alice Austen was alive today, she'd be a medical miracle."

"Lesbians from the grave!" said TJ. "Now that is a horror film I'd watch."

I put on my backpack, grabbed a third cookie, and stood up. "We hate to eat and run, but—"

"Where are we going?" TJ asked.

"Where do you think we're going? To Ms. Hansen for more information!"

TJ swiped another cookie too and followed me out the door.

I bypassed the slow-as-a-tortoise elevator and ran down and around the three flights of marble stairs, left hand poised an inch from the handrail, to grab on if I lost balance, but otherwise letting the tips of my toes rat-a-tat-tat my way down. At the bottom of each flight, I grabbed on to the banister and used my momentum to swoop myself around 180 degrees so I could run down the hall to the next set of steps. At the bottom, three wide stairs opened out into the main lobby. There I ate my last cookie while waiting for TJ, who finally appeared, having enjoyed theirs on the way down.

I rang Ms. Hansen's bell, then bounced slightly on the bristle welcome mat. It barely still read THERE'S NO PLACE LIKE HOME in a swirling font. TJ stood behind me.

"Who is it?" Ms. Hansen called out melodically.

"It's Sam. Sam Marino, from 5-C."

"And TJ Williams from down the block."

The tingling of a chain lock and the heavy *ka-chunk* of a dead bolt later, Ms. Hansen opened the door. She was an extremely short woman wearing a rainbow tie-dyed T-shirt and black leggings, with powder-gray curly hair, veiny hands, and a growing smile on her face. Nacious was at her ankles, dancing around.

"We have some questions," I announced.

"Questions?" Ms. Hansen raised her eyebrows.

"Questions."

"If you're not busy," TJ added.

"Not at all. Come on in."

Nacious made a circle around us and then trotted over to where her leash hung on the wall.

"Sorry, buddy," said TJ, bending down to scratch her head. "We're not going out right now." Nacious settled down on the ground with her paws and chin resting on the floor in disappointment.

"Can I get you some lemonade?" asked Ms. Hansen.

"Yes, please," TJ and I said together. Cookies *and* lemonade? Hanging out with adults who weren't your parents sure had its advantages.

"Have a seat at the table. I'll be right there."

Ms. Hansen's place was like my and Jess's apartments, so

the kitchen was too small to eat in. Instead, the main room was split into a dining area with a retro rounded metal table and chair set and a living area with a simple couch across from a boxy, old television. Ms. Hansen had decorated the walls with shelves of knickknacks, including a section dedicated to salt and pepper shakers and a display of sixty small spoons in five rows of twelve. The overhead light was on, but it was still pretty dim in the living room, as if the clutter on the walls sucked up the light.

A hallway led down to two bedrooms and, at the end, the bathroom. I had been back there a few times, when I really had to go after walking Nacious, but the two bedroom doors were always closed. I had wondered before which bedroom Ms. Hansen slept in and what she did with the other one. Now I wondered whether she had once lived with someone else, and whether that someone was another woman, maybe her partner.

"Here you go!"

I was so deep in thought that I jumped a bit at Ms. Hansen's cheery voice as she placed three tall glasses on the table, the ice in two of them still spinning from having been stirred. Ms. Hansen knew that I preferred my drinks without *rocks*, as she called them.

"Sorry, I don't have anything to go with it. I'm no baker like Jess."

"You know Jess bakes?"

"Why, of course I do. Before she and Val had—oh golly, what's the baby's name again?"

"Evie."

"Right, Evie. Before Evie was born, she was always dropping off some treat or another. It's just starting to pick up again, and I don't know how she does it."

Huh. I never knew Jess brought baked goods to Ms. Hansen.

"So, you said you had questions?"

"Well, we were doing some research for a history project on a local figure," TJ began, "and we've come across someone quite interesting . . ."

I couldn't wait for TJ's sibling-developed fancy dance talk. I took over and got right to it. "Did you know Alice Austen? And was she really a lesbian?"

"Excuse me?" Ms. Hansen's eyes grew wide, punctuated by several large blinks.

TJ jabbed my side with their elbow. "What Sam means is, we were researching this photographer, Alice Austen."

Ms. Hansen had started to nod slowly. "I remember Alice. I just wasn't expecting to hear her name out of your mouths. Or this century, to be honest. And yes, she was one hundred percent a lesbian."

"How do you know?" I winced at my own question the

moment I asked it, but if it was rude, Ms. Hansen hadn't seemed to notice.

"Well, I don't know whether she'd have used the word herself." Ms. Hansen looked up at the ceiling in thought. "Not everyone felt comfortable with words back then that are just fine today. But if you saw her with Gertrude for more than two minutes, you'd know. Alice used to say she lived *the larky lifestyle.*"

"The what?" I asked.

"Basically, being a bohemian."

"Again, not to be rude, but—what??"

"I think she means like being a weirdo," said TJ.

Ms. Hansen nodded in agreement.

"Oh! Cool! So you knew her?"

"I did, I did." Ms. Hansen nodded as she repeated herself, in that way that old people do when they're trying to hunt back in the closet of their memories for a sweater they haven't worn in a long time. "She lived here back when I was little. My family moved in when I was just three years old, you know, and I've lived here since then." She beamed with pride. "Anyway, I was your age when she moved here with Gertrude, maybe a bit younger. They were only here a few years, and they were old at the time, probably about as old as I am now, come to think of it. They were the first women I ever knew who lived and loved like that."

"And, um, Jess was saying that you might *live the larky life-style* too?" It wasn't really a question, but I lifted my voice and eyebrow in hopes that Ms. Hansen would respond as if it were.

She laughed. "I've been wondering when that would come up. In fact, I thought that's what your first question was going to be about."

"We're queer too," TJ added. "We're not, like, judging you or anything."

"Well, I don't know about *larky*, but that's me, Les the les, in the flesh."

TJ looked as confused as I did.

"My first name is Leslie," Ms. Hansen said.

"Ohhhhh, right!" I said, remembering that Jess had called her that.

"The first hundred times I heard *Les the les*, it was from kids on the playground, way before I knew what a lesbian was or that I was one."

"That sucks," said TJ.

"It sure did. I even had a couple of years in high school where I started going by my middle name just to avoid it. But people called me a lesbian anyway, and by college, I knew that they were right. Pretty soon I was Les the les, in the flesh, and I haven't looked back!"

"Wow," said TJ. "I can't imagine not knowing I was queer until college."

"And compared to a lot of other people my age, I came out early." Leslie raised her eyebrows high, as if she were the one surprised to hear it. "Things were different back then. Everyone was expected to be straight, and if you weren't, you certainly didn't want anyone to know about it. I even had a boyfriend in high school, and we went to the prom together. I heard from him years later, and it turned out he was gay too."

"Did you ever have a girlfriend?" I asked.

"Lots!" said Leslie with a surprisingly sly grin. "Especially once the gay liberation movement kicked into gear in the seventies. There were women loving women everywhere! Well, comparatively, that is. It was still in the bars mostly, and you had to be careful on your way there and home. You couldn't hold hands with your partner, or walk too close to them. And even if you were by yourself, it could be dangerous if you didn't look like what people expected straight people to look like."

"That sounds awful!" I said. I never worried when I walked around, just being myself. From the wrinkles of disgust on TJ's face, they agreed.

Leslie nodded. "It wasn't ideal. But it was what we did to get by. You were probably okay in the Village, but by the time you got to the subway, you had better fit in."

"What village?" asked TJ.

"Why, Greenwich Village, of course!" Leslie said with a

flutter of her hands. "Home of New York City's queer culture."

I had heard of Greenwich Village before, which was pronounced like *Gren-Itch*, but I'd never heard anyone who talked about it quite so casually, as if it were home.

"I used to go to Brooklyn a bit, especially for women's events, but mostly it was Manhattan."

"Did you ever go to the Pride Center of Staten Island?" I asked.

Leslie laughed. "That place is younger than you two! The Center in Manhattan only started in the eighties."

I'd been to The Center in the city with Jess. It was a huge old building that I thought had always been there, or at least for more than forty years. Forty years was a lot of time when I thought about being twelve years old, but it wasn't there for the entire first half of Leslie's life.

"It really makes you admire people like Alice and Gertrude," Leslie continued. "They managed a fifty-plus-year relationship in a time when people ignored their love at best, and the only culture they had that reflected themselves was the one they made with their friends."

"Wow," I said.

"Yeah," said Leslie. "Wow. The days of life are slow, but how fast the years can go and the change they bring."

The three of us sat in the pleasant, timeless quiet, finishing our lemonade together, until TJ's phone buzzed. "I gotta go," they said. "I'm on for dinner help tonight. But thanks for the lemonade, Ms. Hansen. And for sharing with us."

"Call me Leslie. Only straight people call me Ms. Hansen." Leslie winked.

"Okay, Leslie."

"Yeah, thanks, Leslie." I tipped back the last syrupy-sweet bit of tangy liquid onto my tongue.

On the elevator up to my apartment, I thought about knowing queer people on the first, fourth, and fifth floors. And maybe there were queer people on the second and third floors too. No more assuming people were straight, not even old people.

I dropped off my bag and shoes and went right to the long windowsill in my room. Alice Austen had once lived in this apartment. Maybe she even slept in this room, alongside Gertrude. And in the daytime, maybe she'd stare out at the water and think about how her view had changed. She was poor by then, and near the end of her life, but maybe she could still see the copper statue in the water, which had turned green, and maybe she would think about how she had lived her life with the freedom and determination of a person wearing a crown and holding a torch in the air.

CHAPTER NINE

"Annnnnnnnd send!" I pushed the button to print out our report. Any other teacher would have had us submit through the school portal online, but Watras demanded (in his words) a "real live piece of paper." He had not been pleased when Rebekkah pointed out that paper is made up of dead trees and plant matter, so it's not alive.

"There's just one thing left," said TJ.

"What else do we need to do? We already practiced our presentation three times. How much more ready do you want us to be?"

"A speech is only about a quarter what you say. Most of it"—TJ tugged at the corners of their cadet-blue button-down shirt—"is about style."

"I don't think Watras is going to grade us based on our fashion sense."

"Maybe not, but it'll help us be in the mood to present. Plus, it'll be more fun."

"More fun for who?"

"For both of us, if you'd get into it. I mean, we have to wear something to school anyway. Might as well look good."

TJ put on a song by Miss Chris for inspiration and opened my closet with a shimmy of their shoulders. The closet floor was cluttered with a pile of board games and art supplies. The hanging rod was empty except for a few bare hangers and three dresses pushed to one side for when I had to dress up for family events. Dresses weren't great, but they were better than the tie-and-dress-pants alternative. At least dresses were loose at the neck and waist.

"Do you not have a single button-down shirt in your wardrobe?" TJ nearly always wore a button-down shirt. They loved the way a fitted shirt accented the lines of their body.

"Have you ever seen me wear a button-down shirt? You know what happens when I wear a button-down shirt? Peepholes!!"

I pointed down at where a row of buttons would leave a set of awkward diamonds between where the fabric pulled together. Even if the shirt looked safe in the mirror, once I was out and moving, gaps were inevitable.

"Oh. Right. Even if you get a bigger size?"

"If I get a big enough size, the arms are long enough to be pants."

"Okay, okay, no button-downs. I'm still gonna wear one though."

"Wouldn't be very TJ if you didn't."

They went through my dresser with an almost-mechanical *no, no, no*. It was a lot like the *no, no, no* I did when I went through the same clothes, but it felt different hearing it from someone else. More judgy, and I didn't like it.

"You could just wear your own thing and not worry about us coordinating," I pointed out.

"But where's the joy in *that*?"

"Are you filled with joy now?"

TJ just shook their head while Miss Chris transitioned into a slow song about rain falling on a round window. They pulled out a black polo shirt with small white polka dots. "This could be good. It's even got a collar."

"Let me see it." I liked the shirt but hadn't worn it since the spring because the fabric was too heavy for summer. I'd have to check it to make sure it still fit okay. I hadn't noticed other clothes not fitting recently, but with a fat body, you never know. Jess always tried on an outfit before going out with Val, even before she was pregnant.

Jess also changed her shirt right in front of me. She always turned her back but said it was important for fat kids to see fat bodies, and that I was welcome to close my eyes if I didn't feel comfortable. I had gotten used to the sight of Jess's body, but that didn't mean I was going to change in front of someone, especially not someone thin like TJ, best friend or not.

"I'll be right back."

I dashed to the bathroom and changed into the polka-dot shirt, which fit great. I switched back into the gray T-shirt with the green apple that had an old woman's face and gray beehive hair, sandwiched between the words GRANNY SMITH HAS APPEAL! and gave TJ a thumbs-up when I got back to the bedroom, tossing the polo shirt on the bed.

"I didn't even get to see it on you." TJ picked up the shirt and turned it right side out to fold it.

"Who are you, my mother?"

TJ lifted their voice in a rough approximation of a cartoon mom. *"Sam, I just want to make sure you put your best foot forward."*

"My mom has never once sounded like that. It's much more *Sam, I spent good money on that clothing, and the least you can do is respect it and me by treating it well.*" I copied TJ's cartoon mom voice.

"I mean, she's not wrong." TJ picked it up and gave it a couple of shakes. "It needs an ironing."

"I thought only button-down shirts needed ironing. That's another reason I don't have any."

"Look at it. It's all wrinkled, and the collar is bent on one side."

TJ was right. I hadn't really looked at the shirt in the mirror when I tried it on. I had been focused on whether it fit, was comfortable, and covered my stomach, even if I raised my hands. What can I say? That's what I'm looking for in clothing.

"Does your mom have an iron?" asked TJ.

"How should I know?"

TJ headed off and returned a few minutes later with a cordless iron and a bath towel.

"She said you broke the ironing board a couple of years ago and that neither of you wears enough ironed clothing to replace it."

"Oh, that's right! I was sitting on it and trying to pull the lever so that it would collapse under me, like a low-budget amusement park ride. I guess we do have an iron."

TJ shook their head and said "Bless your heart" the way their grandma did when she wanted to say that TJ had just said something ridiculous.

When TJ finished ironing the shirt, they hung it in the closet. "And make sure to wear it to school. Don't just stuff it in your backpack to pull out right before class, or it'll get all wrinkled again."

"Yes, Mother."

"Watch who you're gendering, nonbinary offspring!"

"Yes, genderfluid parental figure."

"That's better!"

With TJ's style bug satisfied, we flopped onto my bed.

"I still can't believe she really lived here. HERE!" TJ practically vibrated with excitement.

"They. Gertrude was here too!"

"They might have slept there! Or there! Or there!" TJ pointed around the room.

"Or even right here!" I added.

TJ jumped, which was a little silly because it had been a long time ago.

"They cooked in my kitchen!"

"They sat in your living room!"

"They took showers in my bathroom!"

"They pooped in your toilet!"

"Ew!"

"Sorry. The Littles have really been into potty humor lately, and now I keep thinking about poop jokes. How about some Mx. Liberty trivia instead? I learned a good one."

"Bring it on."

"Do you know why we got them?"

"That's easy," I said. "France gave them to us."

"Yeah, but why?"

The video I had watched a few weeks ago with Jess had talked about how the statue had been built and their life in the water, but it hadn't gone into detail about where they came from. Or, if it had, I had still been eating brownies at the time and wasn't really paying attention yet. "Wasn't it about immigration?"

"Nope! It *became* a symbol of immigration. But it was originally about celebrating the end of slavery. There are even broken chains on their feet." TJ pulled out their phone, pulled up an image, and gave it to me. The picture was a close-up of broken chains by the statue's massive sandaled left foot, its giant toes poking out from behind layers of green copper fabric.

"Oh wow! This is seriously cool."

"I know. That's why they're called the Statue of *Liberty*. As in freedom from slavery. After I got my dad with that question about which hand their book is in, he did some research. It turns out the Lady honors his side of my family, not my mom's."

"I can't believe they didn't mention it in the video." Brownies or no brownies, I would have remembered this.

"I can. White people have been taking credit for things by, for, and about Black people for four hundred years. It's rock 'n' roll all over again."

"Sharp!"

"More like flat!"

"Good one!"

Trivia complete, we went back to naming things Alice and Gertrude might have done in my apartment until the barking alarm rang on my phone.

After Nacious's walk, Leslie invited us in for lemonade and asked us how our report went.

"The essay's really good," I told her. "Or at least I think it is, and TJ did an amazing job on the artwork."

"I'd love to see it," said Leslie. "That is, if you don't mind, of course."

"We need to bring TJ's drawing to school," I said, "but I can email you the rest when I get upstairs."

"I'm sure you did a great job on it, and I look forward to reading your take on Alice."

"We're not really done until we present it in class though," TJ added. "Which means that if we don't go tomorrow, we're going to have to pick out new outfits."

I groaned. I couldn't help it. TJ sounded far too pleased about the prospect.

"We can go upstairs and pick out a backup now," TJ offered with a too-bright smile that said they knew I wouldn't want to.

"No thanks." If we presented on Monday, we wouldn't need a backup outfit.

"We could wear matching dresses." TJ cheesed a grin.

"Fat chance!" I said, and slapped my stomach. Jess taught me that one.

"I haven't worn a dress in"—Leslie looked up at the ceiling while ticking off decades on her long, bony fingers—"ten, twenty, thirty—oh boy! Over forty years now! I remember because it was my father's funeral and I was a forty-year-old woman fighting with my mother over what I was wearing and I swore I'd never let myself down like that again."

"Wow!" said TJ.

"It got easier once the seventies hit and there were more androgynous clothes around. And nowadays, why, just check out the two of you!"

I looked down at my sparkly sneakers, gray sweatpants, and apple T-shirt, and over at TJ in their blue button-down, blue jeans, and red canvas shoes.

"I mean, with the three-piece rule and everything, sometimes I'd wear a woman's blouse to the bars, just to make life a little easier on myself." Leslie put up her hands in a gesture of resignation. "It was just one less thing to worry about."

"Three-piece rule? Is that like the five-second rule?"

Leslie laughed. "I wish. You mean your queer mentors never told you about the three-piece rule?"

"Who?"

"Jess and Val. The cute couple with the baby."

"They're not my mentors," I said. "They're my friends."

Leslie paused, mouth open, then shook her head, as if to herself.

"So what's the three-piece rule?" asked TJ.

"The three-piece rule was when the police said you had to

wear three pieces of clothing from the 'correct' gender." Leslie made air quotes around the word *correct*. "If you didn't, you could be arrested, right here in New York City."

"Arrested?!" TJ sounded as shocked as I felt.

"But who can say what your correct gender is?" I asked.

"And what if your correct gender is nonbinary?" asked TJ.

Leslie let out a sound somewhere between a chuckle and a sigh. "Cops with batons got to say what they wanted, and *nonbinary* was not in their playbook."

TJ and I looked at each other in horror.

"Do you kids even know about Stonewall?"

"Of course we do," I said. Val had told me about it. Police came to raid a gay bar in Manhattan, and there were riots and it started the modern gay rights movement and the Pride Parade.

"So you know about the GLF?"

"The GLF?" I asked.

"The Gay Liberation Front. It started right after Stonewall, to continue the work for gay rights. And what about Sylvia Rivera and Marsha P. Johnson and STAR?"

"I've heard of Sylvia Rivera," I said. She was a gender-nonconforming trans rights activist. Jess and Val even had a small picture of her in their living room, wearing a sweater and heels as she leaned against a heavy bulk of metal on a city pier.

"Me too," said TJ. "But not Marsha P. Johnson. And what's STAR?"

"Sylvia and Marsha P. were the cofounders of STAR—Street Transvestite Action Revolutionaries," said Leslie with reverence.

"Transvestite?" I asked. As far as I knew, that was an offensive word.

"Language changes, remember," said Leslie. "I wouldn't call someone that now, but that was the language they used for themselves. They were downright stunning, in body and thought. As in, those queens literally stunned people, left them with their mouths agape as they passed by. They knew it, and they loved it. And they used it to push for trans and homeless rights. They had been homeless themselves, and brought homeless trans youth into their home whenever and however they could.

"There's a lot more to queer history than Alice Austen, you know. Alice was amazing to be sure, but she wasn't a queer activist, and she lived in high society for most of her life."

"She and her friends were also all white," added TJ.

"True," said Leslie. "Marsha P. was Black and Sylvia was Latinx, and that played a big role in the kind of work they did. STAR only lasted a few years, but they helped so many young, poor, queer youth then and for the rest of their lives, and they inspired many others. In some ways, if they didn't do the work they did, you wouldn't be able to live now the way you do."

"Sorry," I said. "I wish I knew more."

"No, no." She shook her hand as well as her head. "It's not your fault. I don't mean to shame you. How are you supposed to know these things if no one tells you? And with our community, most of us are raised in families that don't know and don't want to know. But Sylvia and Marsha P. changed the world, and it's a shame how few young people know about them. Or any queer history at all. As if being queer is something new."

That line echoed in my head for the rest of the day. If we could get a statue of *The Darned Club* at Borough Hall, people passing by would have to know there have always been LGBTQIAP+ people on Staten Island, no matter what they called themselves. The next day's presentation had become even more important.

CHAPTER TEN

Monday morning, TJ and I were ready. TJ was wearing a black button-down with white piping and pearlescent buttons to match my black polo shirt, but where I had on black stretch pants and my regular sparkly sneakers, TJ wore velveteen pants and shiny black shoes they called classy oxfords. The principal even complimented us on our outfits on the way into the building.

"See?" said TJ. "Making a stylish impression matters."

I shrugged. I didn't mind wearing the shirt if it made TJ happy, but I wasn't about to try winning people over with my fashion sense.

Watras greeted the class with a rare grin. "Welcome to report week, ladies and gentlemen!"

TJ and I exchanged a glance of shared irritation. The school code said that you weren't supposed to refer to students by gender like that, but when we had brought it up to Watras, he had barely given a whiff of an apology followed by a lengthy explanation of his age and experience. It was worse than being called *ladies and gentlemen* in the first place.

"I am excited to hear your reports, and to choose one to enter into the borough-wide battle to become a real statue in front of Borough Hall." He said it like it was the beginning of the world's most boring television competition show, called *So You Think You're a Locally Relevant Historical Figure*.

"Since we will be focused on hearing your reports this week, you will not need to sit in your regular seats." A smattering of cheers speckled the room. "Instead, sit with your project partner. Choose one spot for the week and stay there."

The room filled with the screeches and thunks of thirty-two middle school students rearranging themselves, along with hopeless cries from Watras that this process did not require extensive use of the mouth muscles. I was already at the end of my row, so TJ took the seat next to me and we were done. We even had time for a round of Super-Tic-Tac-Toe on a four-by-four board before the rest of the class worked out which pairs of friends were going to sit next to which other pairs of friends.

The way Watras did oral reports, seating aside, was awful. He wouldn't let students volunteer to go first like any other teacher would. He wanted everyone to be ready on day one and somehow he thought that the best way to accomplish this was to put everyone's name in a glass fishbowl and, in his words, *let fate set the agenda.*

Alanna and Sarah presented first, and to no one's surprise, their statue subject was Alexander Hamilton, even though he'd lived in Manhattan, not Staten Island. Sarah said that since there were a number of his descendants on the island, there was a local connection. Watras did not look convinced.

Josh and Abe's statue model was pretty cool, a drawing of a man standing on a bridge. He was the same size as the bridge and stood with his head held high and his fisted hands on his hips.

"Do you know which bridge this is?" asked Abe. There are four bridges to get onto—or off of—Staten Island.

"The Verrazzano!"

"Bayonne!"

"Goethals!"

"No, no, and no!" said Abe proudly.

"Oh! It's the other one! All the way down on the south shore!"

"The Outerbridge!"

"Correct!" said Josh. "But get this. It's not called that because of where it is, even though you'd think so. It's officially called the Outerbridge Crossing, and that's because of Eugenius Outerbridge, the person we picked for our presentation. Can you believe that? His *name* was Outerbridge, and they named the bridge farthest from Manhattan after him! How cool is that?" Josh went on to tell the class about Outerbridge, the first chairman of the Port Authority, which runs the bridges, tunnels, piers, and airports in the New York City area. The report itself was pretty boring, but Watras nodded approvingly and made notes on his page.

Joanne and Rhyan presented on Frederick Law Olmsted, who had designed both Central Park in Manhattan and Prospect Park in Brooklyn. Sarah wanted to know why he hadn't built a park on Staten Island, but Rhyan said that most of Staten Island was forest back then. When they were done, Joanne handed in their report to Watras, who looked at a tear at the top of the page disapprovingly. That was another terrible thing about Watras: If you handed in homework or a project with bent or ragged edges, he would take points off, even if he hadn't collected it on the first day. I was glad that TJ had our project, because they would have put it somewhere it wouldn't get wrinkled.

Dan and Erik went last for the day with their report on Henry Hudson—so we were four for four on DSCWMs. They had created a pretty good clay sculpture, but their report was still about some settler guy who basically took advantage of the Lenape who were already living here. Dan talked about them like they were just sitting around waiting to guide Hanky boy inland.

"What, is a river not good enough for him?" asked Cara, referring to the waterway that ran along the west side of Manhattan, up to Albany and beyond.

"And the bay too!" Rebekkah added.

"And there's already a statue of Henry Hudson up in the Bronx," said Jason. "He's got a whole dang park up there!"

Watras just waved his hand as a signal to be quiet and made a note in his book.

We weren't called on Monday, so TJ insisted on another outfit consult that night, and again the night after that. Finally, on Wednesday, it was our turn. I wore a loose purple tie over a black T-shirt and TJ wore a black button-down with a pattern of small purple triangles.

Sure enough, when Watras pulled our names out of the bowl first, TJ slipped a plastic folder out of the back of their binder and presented a pristine set of pages. I didn't know how TJ did it, but I was happy they did.

Alice Austen Was a Lesbian

Sam Marino and TJ Williams

Most people on Staten Island have probably heard of Alice Austen. There's even a ferry named after her. But a lot of people don't know who she really was and we want to fix that. We think that she would be a great subject for the new statue at Staten Island Borough Hall, and we believe her picture The Darned Club *would make a wonderful design.*

Alice Austen was born on Staten Island in 1866. She was an early photographer and she spent most of her life at her family home, called Clear Comfort, at 2 Hylan Boulevard, right by the water. Her life partner, Gertrude Tate, joined her there in 1917, after they had already known each other for eighteen years. They had money problems, and in 1945, they lost the house and moved into the same building Sam lives in now, where they lived for four years. In fact, it's the very same apartment! This is an important personal connection for Sam, and for TJ too, especially because we got to interview Leslie Hansen, who lives in the same building and who once knew Alice.

Alice Austen took about eight thousand photographs during her life. That's impressive when you remember that it was at a time when she had to carry fifty pounds of equipment with her and get the people in her pictures to stay still for seconds, or even minutes, while the camera slowly captured the light patterns that made up the image. Plus, she had to develop each plate by hand in her darkroom. She carried her equipment all over Staten Island, and then all over Europe, taking photographs everywhere she could, but her favorite thing to shoot were the ships that passed right in front of her house, entering and leaving New York Harbor.

For our statue design, we picked a picture that Alice took with her friends in front of her home. She is on the left in the photograph. We chose this image because it represents friendship, which is something that we, and Staten Islanders in general, care a lot about.

We also chose this image because it celebrates women being close to each other. Alice Austen was a lesbian, and we think it's important for Staten Islanders to celebrate LGBTQIAP+ history. A lot of people think of the LGBTQIAP+ community as new. We thought so too, until we learned about Alice and talked with Leslie. This statue would promote visibility for the LGBTQIAP+ community now, in the past, and in the future.

When Gertrude was 75, she got severe bronchitis and couldn't take care of Alice anymore. She moved back to her family in Queens, who still disapproved of her relationship with Alice. Alice moved to an assisted living facility and died in 1952. They were both very lonely at the end of their lives. We think it is terrible that Gertrude's family didn't support them and help them spend Alice's last days together. We believe that a statue of The Darned Club would help make it so that no one's family disapproves of their relationship because of the gender of the person they love.

Out of more than a hundred sculptures in New York City recogniz-
ing historical figures, fewer than ten are of women, and we think that's
wrong. Alice Austen represents Staten Island, and we hope that you
will choose her for your project. It's time Ms. Liberty had someone to
talk to.

I read the first three paragraphs to the class. I was glad I got to share the part about Alice and Leslie living in my building. Meanwhile, TJ hung a big copy of Alice's photograph and their pencil sketch of what *The Darned Club* would look like as a statue.

Then it was TJ's turn to read. I looked around the room and there were plenty of kids drawing in their notebooks and maybe not paying attention, but I did see some kids smiling and whispering to each other when TJ read the part about LGBTQIAP+ people. When it was time for questions, lots of kids rose their hands.

"How did you find out that she was a lesbian?" asked Abe.

"She didn't use that word, as far as we know, and she might have been bisexual, but if you look at her pictures and read about her life with her partner, Gertrude, you can tell she wasn't straight, and people around her knew it," I said.

"Did she take that picture herself?" asked Joanne.

"She sure did!" said TJ. "She set it all up and used a remote trigger to press the button on her camera."

"Cool! Selfie!" said Rhyan.

"Do you think it'll bother straight people to pass by a statue like that?" asked Erik.

The room got silent, except for one person sucking their teeth, and then a pencil hitting the floor. Whoever dropped it didn't move to pick it up.

I looked at TJ. TJ looked at me. My mouth opened first, but it could have been either of us talking.

"You know what?" I said. "I don't really care. I mean, I walk past statues of straight men all the time and no one asks whether it bothers me. And it kinda does. Not, like, that there are statues of straight men. But sometimes it seems like there are *only* statues of straight men."

"Didn't you hear that part I read about it being important for queer people like us to see ourselves in culture too?" TJ added.

"Okay," said Watras. "That'll be enough questions. Interesting choice." He said *interesting* in that adult way that said *yuck* and pulled another slip of paper from the bowl. "Sonia and Liz, you're next."

Their presentation on Aaron Burr annoyed Sarah, but Sonia pointed out that Burr had died on Staten Island, so he had local relevance, and that while Lin-Manuel Miranda had made him out to be the enemy, he was actually an important historical figure. Then Watras shook his head at Anthony and Jason's report on the Wu-Tang Clan, even though, as Jason pointed out, they had been pumping out jam after jam since 1992, which definitely counted as being in the last century.

Watras released us thirty seconds before the bell with the air of a fairy godfather granting some great wish.

Rhyan and Joanne came up to TJ and me as we were getting our things together.

"That was cool, what you said to Erik about not really caring what people think," said Joanne.

"Thanks," I said,

"Yeah," said Rhyan. "And that statue's awesome! I'd love to pass by it on the way to the ferry."

Joanne nodded. "My aunt's dating a woman, and I think it would be really nice for them to see it too. I wonder if they even know about Alice Austen."

"We didn't before we started this project," said TJ, "but her photographs are amazing."

"Anyway," said Joanne, "good luck!"

"You too," TJ and I said in unison.

Joanne's aunt got me to thinking that maybe Watras

knew someone queer, or maybe he was even queer him-self, and that his gruffness today was just regular Watras behavior. Maybe Watras wanted to see more LGBTQIAP+ representation on Staten Island too. Maybe we could really win this thing.

CHAPTER ELEVEN

Watras didn't mention the projects on Thursday, and on Friday, all he said was that he was nearly finished writing up his notes and finalizing our grades.

On Monday, the words WATRAS'S WINNERS were written on the right side of the whiteboard with a blank space below it, where there was usually a (supposedly) inspirational quote.

It was a "traditional lecture" class, and the minutes passed as slowly as they ever had. It was like Watras had written the words just to remind us that he hadn't given back our projects yet. If it had been anyone else, I would have been surprised. Finally, two minutes before the bell rang, Watras pulled the stack of reports out of his bag and started handing all but one of them back. He hung the last one up on the right side of the whiteboard with a magnet.

"Henry Hudson?!" called out Rhyan.

"YES!" Dan and Erik high-fived.

"Are you kidding me?!" yelled TJ.

Rhyan was not kidding. There was Erik and Dan's project, with a red 95 circled at the top. And ours was in my hand, with a 93. I dropped the paper facedown onto my desk.

"You may move around quietly to check in with your partner." The room filled with the scrapes of dozens of tables and chairs, nearly drowning out the rest of Watras's sentence. "But do not leave the classroom until the bell rings."

"A ninety-three?" TJ mouthed with exaggerated lips.

"I know!" I said. "We were so close!"

We flipped to the back page, where Watras had stapled our score breakdown. We got:

Subject choice: 15/15

Statue design: 11/15

Statue model: 14/15

Essay content: 19/20

Essay grammar: 15/15

Presentation: 19/20

Comments:

Watras never wrote anything in the comments section.

"We lost four points for statue design," TJ hissed.

"That's more than half of the points we lost. And what does that even mean? I thought your statue was amazing!"

"It was. Look—we got fourteen out of fifteen for the model itself. It's the design that was the problem." TJ stopped and their face fell. "The design of queer women hugging each other."

Now it was my turn to hiss. "That absolute—"

The bell rang through my expletive, and Watras dismissed the class with a resigned wave. Most kids fled for the relative freedom of the hallway, but TJ and I approached his desk. He was writing in a thick notebook and acted like we weren't there.

"Could we talk to you for a minute?" I asked once the last of the other students had left. It was remarkable how quiet the large room felt with just my voice in it.

Watras held up a finger as he continued writing for another two lines before putting down his pen and looking up at us. "Yes?"

I looked over at TJ. It was their turn to let their voice echo.

"We . . . um . . . wanted to talk with you about our entry into the statue contest."

"Alice Austen, right?" Watras said it like he was performing a feat of memory, but TJ was holding the report in their hand, with their drawing of *The Darned Club* facing him. "It was a solid report."

"But you marked us way low on statue design, and it made us lose."

"Like I said, it was a solid report. And it must have been exciting, Sam, to learn that she lived in your apartment. But it was not a perfect project, and I can only have one winner. I am responsible for choosing the absolute best entry I received."

"Mr. Watras, does Alice Austen's sexuality make you uncomfortable?" TJ asked.

"Not one bit." He cleared his throat in a way that said that it bothered him at least a little. "It's simply that the sculpture you designed doesn't represent Staten Island at the time in the way I was hoping for. You did a great job with your art, TJ, but I just couldn't see it in front of Borough Hall. Perhaps if you had used imagery from one of Austen's street scenes. Newsboys with papers for sale, immigrants in shawls. Something like that might have been more evocative of the era."

"Those pictures aren't even from Staten Island. They were taken in Manhattan."

"Well, I'm delighted to see that you learned so much for this project. It shows that you deserve the high score you got."

"But Henry Hudson already has so much named after him."

"He was an important man. Don't you think people deserve to know about the namesake of the river and bay they live by? Erik and Dan's essay was inspiring. Ms. Austen has a ferry, as you pointed out in your report, and that's quite an honor."

"But . . ."

"I'm sorry."

"You're not sorry. You're not sorry at all."

"Now, Sam."

"This is our project, and we worked hard on it."

"Dan and Erik worked hard on their project too. I'm not going to take anything away from them just because you're being a squeaky wheel. My decision is final. Now get to your next class before this becomes a *problem*."

Watras opened the classroom door, and a few students for the next period entered before we could get through.

I was angry at Watras for picking Dan and Erik's project, and I was angry at myself for being foolish enough to think, even for a minute, that Watras would have picked us for the highest grade in the class. And no matter what he said, I knew it was because we picked an image of women hugging each other. We could have written a ten-page paper and he still would have picked Henry Hudson.

I wanted to scream. I wanted to cry. But most of all, I wanted to share Alice with all of Staten Island.

"How was school?" Mom set a heavy tuna casserole dish in the center of the table at dinner that night.

"Like being trampled on by an elephant parade."

"That good, huh?" said Mom.

"Watras is totally unfair!"

"That's your science teacher, right?" said Mom. "No, wait. Social studies."

"US History."

"Same difference." I'm pretty sure that was one of the most annoying things a person could say. If you are acknowledging that there's a difference between two things, they're no longer the same.

Mom continued. "So what did Mr. Watras do that was so unfair?"

"So you know that statue project on Alice Austen that TJ and I have been working on?"

"You've barely talked about anything else for two weeks."

"But she lived in THIS apartment. THIS APARTMENT!"

"I know, and that is very cool, but it doesn't mean you have to yell at me."

"Sorry." I hadn't meant to yell *at* Mom. I was yelling because Watras was so terrible and Mom just happened to be in front of my mouth at the time. I took a few breaths and tried again. "We got our projects back, and some dumb statue of Henry Hudson won."

"Well, that's too bad," Mom said, with none of the indignation I was expecting, or at least hoping for.

"You don't understand!"

"What I understand is that another group got a higher score. Sometimes you don't win. It happens."

"But Watras was biased against Alice Austen because she was a lesbian."

"What proof do you have of that?"

"He said he didn't think the image of two pairs of women was representative of Staten Island. What's that supposed to mean? He hates gay people."

"Sam, I think you're jumping to conclusions. I know, you put a lot of work into this project, but so did other kids in your class, and just because you do a great job doesn't always mean you win."

"I'm going downstairs."

I stepped into my fuzzy slippers and ran down to 4-E. I knocked and then opened the door. Or at least I tried to. The door was locked, since I had been too angry to text in advance. So I knocked again, louder this time.

"Hello?" Jess's voice sounded strange behind the door, in that way someone you know well sounds just a little bit different when they're talking to someone they don't know.

"It's me!" When the bolt didn't immediately turn in the lock, I added, "Sam!"

"Oh! Hi, Sam. Just give me a minute."

I counted to myself and reached 103 before Jess finally opened the door. Nearly two minutes.

"Sorry, were you feeding Evie?"

"No, I was just . . . *au naturel.*"

"You were where?"

"In my birthday suit. Nude. Naked. Clothing-free."

"Okay, okay, I get it."

"So, what brings you banging at my door with no warning?"

"Our history teacher didn't pick our project for the statue contest! And I would've texted you before I came down, but Mom took his side and got me all mad." The words tumbled out like a waterfall.

"Okay . . ." Jess nodded slowly, which only made me want to talk faster.

"And then Watras said that our project wasn't representative of Staten Island. Can you even believe it?"

"To be honest, I can."

"What?!" I had kind of expected Mom wouldn't get it. But Jess?

"Sorry, Sam, but you've been complaining about this guy since September. Did you really think he was going to give you the highest score in the class? I mean, it sucks, but I wouldn't get too worked up over it. Who cares what some teacher you don't like anyway says."

"Jess! The project he chose was for Henry Hudson. Henry *freakin'* Hudson!"

"Great!"

"What?"

"Look at it this way. He's only one history teacher out of how many on Staten Island? The odds that his choice would win were already minimal. And with a tired DSCWM like that, now he *really* doesn't have a chance."

"Are you saying our project never had a chance?"

"I'm not saying that," said Jess. "It was a great opportunity to learn about an early lesbian photographer. And it's super cool that she lived in your apartment. But did I think that they were going to make a statue of *The Darned Club*?" Jess sighed. "No, not really."

"I thought best friends were supposed to believe in each other."

Jess's silence said too much.

"Jess?"

"Sam, sweetie." Jess put her hand on my shoulder, but I shook it off.

"Don't call me sweetie."

"That's fair," said Jess. "But, Sam, Val is my best friend."

"And TJ is mine!" I said. "But you can have more than one best friend, can't you?"

"You *can*." Jess drew out the word.

"But I'm not yours."

"Sam, I care a lot about you."

"But we're not best friends."

"You're twelve."

"We're not best friends."

"No, we're not."

The air grew warm as the room filled with an invisible fog. My breath went shallow, and sweat started to form at the corners of my forehead. I stood up and felt wavy.

"I have . . ." My eyes stung, and the corners of my face twitched. "I have to go."

I took a heavy step and then another, wading through the thickness toward the door.

Jess's voice called my name in a way that said *don't go* but from so far away that I couldn't imagine staying.

I pulled the door closed behind me and ran back upstairs, carrying my heart in my hands.

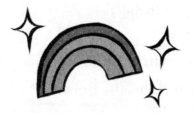

CHAPTER TWELVE

Erik and Dan's report continued to hang on Watras's white-board. And when someone (who might or might not have been me) dragged a finger across the words "We're all rooting for you!" Watras rewrote them fresh. Whoever it was didn't dare try it again, and the words stayed up.

And if that wasn't enough, Erik had discovered that his uncle worked with someone who was on the committee.

"My uncle said that he plans on voting for the best proposal," Erik proclaimed to whoever would listen, "regardless of gender or race, no matter what anyone says. White men shouldn't be at a disadvantage for this competition just because of statues in other places."

"He only says that because he knows it's wrong that most statues are of white men," said Rhyan.

The bell to start class rang before Erik could reply, but the ick of his words hung in the air.

When I got home, I was nervous to go in the building. I was afraid Jess might be in the lobby, and I took the stairs up because I kept picturing her coming out of the elevator when the doors opened. I wasn't planning to talk to Mom about it, at least not yet, but I was in the apartment for less than ten minutes before she brought it up.

"So, are you going down to babysit? It's Tuesday."

"No."

Mom studied me carefully. "Wow, you're usually so excited to see Jess and Evie. This must be serious."

I shrugged in that way that said, *Yeah, I guess, but I don't want to have to say it because then it'll really be true.*

"Something happened, didn't it?" Mom guessed.

I sighed a sigh to sigh down a house made of straw. Maybe even sticks.

"That bad, huh?"

I nodded. I didn't cry often, but when I did, it was an event. My body shook and my nose filled with snot and my lungs had to fight for air with huge, loud gasps. Mom took my hand in hers and squeezed.

"Do you want me to rub your back?"

I started to shake my head. Mom hadn't rubbed my back

in years. But then another round of tears started up. "Yes, please." My voice was smaller than I could believe.

"You know she doesn't hate you, right?" said Mom.

"I . . ." I ran out of air immediately. I took another couple of breaths and tried again. "I don't think she does."

"Well, I know she doesn't."

"How can you be sure?" I sniffled.

"She emailed me this morning to ask how you're doing."

"Oh." That sounded nice, sort of. Then my eyes popped open. "Did she tell you what happened?"

"A bit, but why don't you tell me in your words?"

"I made a *fool* of myself."

"I hate to disappoint you, but if that was your intention, I think you failed."

"What are you talking about?"

"Jess didn't give me a lot of details, but she told me that you talked about friendships and that she said something that really hurt you."

"She said she wasn't my best friend!"

"Oh." Mom stopped rubbing my back and let her hand rest there. "That does sound like a lot to take in."

"It is."

"But isn't TJ your best friend?"

"Yeah, but . . ." I wanted to say a million things, but I wasn't quite sure what any of them were, so I stopped midsentence.

"Take some time to cool off, but I promise, Jess still cares about you." Mom patted my back a few times and smoothed out my shirt. "You need anything?"

"No."

"Do you want anything?"

I wanted a lot. I wanted a heck of a lot. But we didn't have any *Your Best Friend Isn't Your Best Friend* vitamins or *Your Teacher Picked a Different Report* gel, so I shook my head. Mom offered to stay, but all I wanted to do was lie on my floor and listen to Miss Chris.

TJ and I were pretty depressed all week about the outcome of the project. Over the weekend too. TJ didn't even come over for a sleepover on Saturday.

It wasn't the grade. A 93 is a great grade, as Mom reminded me whenever she saw me sulking, which was a lot. It was that TJ and I had felt so proud and happy when we were working on it, thinking about Staten Islanders learning about Alice Austen and queer history. Back when they were alive, people tried to ignore that Alice and Gertrude were lifelong partners who loved each other dearly. I thought that maybe it would be different now. But it felt like the Henry Hudsons and other DSCWMs would always be in charge of history, and that the Alice Austens and other LGBTQIAP+ people would always be second-bests in the shadows.

Plus I still felt pretty terrible about Jess, no matter what Mom said about taking time to cool off.

When I went by myself to pick up Nacious for her Sunday walk, Leslie answered the door wearing a black jumper, a bright yellow silk scarf, and a rainbow bead earring. I'm not sure how we never realized she could be queer. I mean, I don't know about fashion, but you'd think TJ would have noticed.

"Why so down in the mouth?" she asked.

"I'm down all over," I said. "TJ too."

"Is that why they're not here?"

"Yeah."

Nacious put her paws up on my knees and cocked her cheery little face, so I put on her harness and we went outside. I tried to throw the ball for her at the grass yard next to the church, but I think she could tell I wasn't in the mood, because she just curled up with the ball whenever she caught it. And when I tried to take it back, she didn't even wrestle me for it. She just let me have it. So I gave up and walked back home, but I wasn't ready to go in yet, so we walked a block in the other direction before heading inside.

Walking helped, at least a little bit. The air was crisp and the sky was bright blue. But soon we were back home, and walking the same block again would just remind me that I'm not allowed to go farther. We could have also walked down the steep hill toward Richmond Terrace, but that would mean coming back up, a misery I would just as soon avoid. I don't even know whether Nacious could manage it with her stubby pug legs. So we went in.

"Care for some tea?" asked Leslie once I let Nacious out of her harness.

I made a *blecch* face.

"Or water, or lemonade. It doesn't have to be tea. I was basically asking if you wanted to talk."

I nodded.

"I thought you might. I turned on my kettle the moment you left."

"But . . ."

"For me! I can like tea even if you don't, and I'll thank you not to make another face about it. I don't make faces about things you like." Her face was still cheery, but her words were tough as steel. "So, lemonade for you?"

"Yes, please."

Moments later, I was sitting across from Leslie, drinking lemonade with just enough tartness to make my tongue tingle.

"So, what's the problem? Is this about that Alice Austen project you've been working on?"

"Partly."

"You didn't win, did you?"

I shook my head.

"That's too bad. It was a fantastic essay. I loved the personal mention. But who knows if Staten Island's ready for such a clearly lesbian image?"

"It is," I said.

"I'm glad you can be that confident. Things are changing so fast, and it's wonderful. I was never out as a teacher. I couldn't have been. Not that I wasn't brave enough. It's that I would have lost my job, and that wouldn't have helped anyone."

"Sometimes people call me brave for being nonbinary. Even my mom. And you know what?"

"What?" Leslie raised an eyebrow before taking a sip of tea.

"I hate it. I'm not brave. Or, at least, I don't feel that way. I just don't feel like a girl or a boy. What's so brave about that?"

Leslie smiled. "I think they mean that you're brave for living the way you feel, instead of hiding it."

"But it's not that I'm brave. Or that you weren't. It's like you said. Things are different now."

"True. When I was a kid, I would never have been allowed to say the word *lesbian* in school, much less turn in a project proposal for a sapphic statue."

"Sapphic?" I said.

"It's an old-timey word for lesbian. And just as language is changing, culture is too, thanks to people like Alice and Gertrude, and plenty of other queer changemakers, and now you two. This statue may not happen, but the push forward continues, and you helped pave the way."

"Thanks," I said self-consciously. I took my last gulp of lemonade.

"But that's not the only thing bothering you, is it?"

"How did you know?"

"Years of experience. People always try to finish off a drink when they want a conversation to end before it should. That's why I like my tea extra hot. It's a little way of saying to myself that I'm going to take the time to see something through."

"Maybe I was just thirsty," I said.

"Do you want some more? Or some water?" Leslie leaned as if to get up.

"No thanks."

She smiled knowingly and settled back into her seat. "That's what I thought. You don't have to share whatever the other thing is, but I wanted you to have the space."

"Jess isn't my best friend!" I flopped my head back and stared at the ceiling.

Leslie tapped my hand a few times and then squeezed it lightly. "Oh, sweetie. No, no, she's not."

Her words shocked me into sitting upright.

"What? You're supposed to tell me that I'm overreacting."

"I'm not *supposed* to do anything except what I believe is right." She flashed a devious grin.

"Oh, but . . . Jess . . . she . . ." I froze. I didn't know what to say next.

And Leslie sat with me in the silence, until I did.

The words came from deep down. "I thought we were so close. She *told* me we were so close." A quick wave of anger splashed over me, then subsided back into sadness. I looked up at Leslie, who was nodding softly.

"You are close, sweetie. Very, very close. But tell me this—are you close with your mom?"

"Yeah."

"Is she your best friend?"

"It's hard to call someone a best friend when she can ground you." I smirked.

"Exactly!" Leslie slapped one palm into the other for emphasis. "You're very close, but the relationship isn't friendship. You might consider Jess your mentor."

"She's not my mentor!"

"You've told me that twice now, and I'm wondering if you can tell me what a mentor is."

"It's for someone who needs help."

"No wonder you don't want a mentor," said Leslie. "Who wants to be needy? A mentor is someone who . . . well . . . yes, helps someone with less experience. But being inexperienced is just one of the parts of being alive. If you don't like the word *mentor*, you could call her *family*."

"I'm not related to Jess. So we're friends. And if we're not best friends, we're not as close as I thought."

"Blood may be thicker than water, but shared community and experience are thicker than both." Leslie smiled in a way that said she knew that I wouldn't understand her, and that just made it more fun for her to say.

"What?!"

"A lot of gays and lesbians have chosen family. Not people you're related to, but people you feel connection with."

"Are we chosen family?"

Leslie paused. "Well, I'm not sure we're family just yet. I mean, you only stopped calling me Ms. Hansen a few weeks ago."

"Oh."

"But someday maybe. And until then, I'll gladly be a mentor. I've had eighty-two years of experience on the planet, and dare I say, it made me a little wiser."

"That would be cool, I guess."

"And that makes you my mentee."

"Someone younger who learns from you?"

"Yes, and also someone who opens my older eyes to new possibilities. Like a statue of two pairs of women embracing, right in front of Borough Hall."

CHAPTER THIRTEEN

A couple of weeks passed, and things got back to normal. TJ stayed at my place on Saturday, and we invented a new dish, which was three rice crackers stacked with grape jelly between them. If I'd been alone, I would have made one of the layers Nutella chocolate hazelnut spread, but TJ was allergic to nuts. TJ's dad called it a jelly rice club when we told him about it, because it has three layers of cracker, like the three pieces of bread in a club sandwich.

I still hadn't talked to Jess. I missed her, and what Leslie had said about chosen queer family made sense, but it was like I had slammed the door in Jess's face and I didn't know how to open it again. I missed Evie and Val too, and having fun with all three of them together. The fact that it was my fault only made it worse.

If Leslie was right—and she was the kind of person who

usually only said something if she was right—Jess wanted to hear from me but was giving me space and I would have to be the one to reach out first. But I didn't want to text Jess, and I certainly didn't want to get a response. Even if it was good, it wasn't going to be "You're right! We're totally besties. I'm soooooo sorry! Let's belly bump!" If I had thought there would be half a chance she would do it, I would have asked my mom to ask Jess to text me, but I had a feeling that would result in some sort of meaningful and annoying conversation about initiative or whatever, and then I'd still have to talk to Jess myself. Ugh.

One day, on the walk home from the bus, TJ's and my phones both chimed that we had new email. We stopped to read what turned out to be the same message.

> To: Sam Marino, TJ Williams
> From: Judy Roberts
> Subject: Congratulations!
>
> Dear Sam and TJ,
> As president of the Staten Island Historians Association, I am delighted to share with you that we have selected Alice Austen as a finalist in our search for a new statue at the entrance to Borough Hall, across from the Staten Island Ferry. Congratulations

for being one of the strongest entries in a crowded field. We received fifty-three nominations from young Staten Island residents like you. The selection committee appreciated your choice of image, as well as the way your essay showed your connection to Alice and her life as a Staten Islander. How exciting to live in her one-time home, Sam.

You will have the opportunity to present your proposal to our Statue Committee, along with the three other finalists. One of these proposals will be chosen and cast in bronze to stand across from the ferry terminal for residents and guests alike to enjoy. We will reach out to you soon with logistics for meeting with the judges.

Congratulations and good luck!

Judy

"What?" I yelled.

"WHAT?" TJ yelled right back at me, and we went at it for a bit like that.

"WHAT?!"

"WHAAAAT?!?!"

"WH-WH-WH-WHAT!!!"

TJ and I jumped up and down and hug-spun in a circle on the sidewalk until we fell down.

"But how?" I asked. "There's no way Watras changed his mind."

"Could it have been Jess?"

I shook my head, but then I grinned. I knew who it was—who it had to be. We ran the last three blocks to my building. TJ got there way ahead of me but needed me to wrestle my key through the outer and inner doors before following me to Leslie's apartment. I knocked and slowed my heavy breathing.

"Was it you?" I asked, the moment Leslie opened the door.

"Lovely to see you, Sam," she said. "Won't you come in? And TJ too! To what do I owe the pleasure?"

We followed Leslie in and sat on the couch.

"Was it you?" I asked again.

"Was it me what?" Leslie asked as she lowered herself back into her glider chair.

"We just got an email from the president of the Staten Island Historians Association!"

"Oh?" Leslie raised her eyes with a look of surprise that hinted that she wasn't exactly as surprised as I might have thought.

"It WAS you!" I yelled.

"You're going to have to get a lot more specific before I confirm or deny anything."

TJ showed her the email.

She nodded as she read, and then a smile peeked out and wouldn't disappear. "Well, would you look at that? It seems

Staten Island is ready to consider a sapphic statue. Or at least the Historians Association is, and that's saying something."

"You entered it without telling us?" I exclaimed.

"Well, I didn't think anything would come of it, and I didn't want to get your hopes up. You two inspired me to give it a go. You don't mind, do you?"

"It's awesome!" said TJ.

"It's amazing!" I said.

"But how is it even possible?" TJ asked. "It had to be entered by a teacher."

"And I am a teacher," said Leslie. "Or, I was for forty years. But I have to say, it wasn't my idea. After we talked about queer family, Sam, I got in touch with Jess. Have you talked with her recently?"

I shook my head.

"She's there for you when you're ready. She really does care about you. And she was the one who read up on the contest and found out that the rules state that any New York City public school teacher could send in your entry with their letter of recommendation, not just *your* New York City public school teacher. And it said nothing about being retired. I figured I owed it to you and the queer community to send it. I just thought I was going to ruffle a few feathers, but here we are. Wow. Wow wow wow."

"So you wrote a letter about us?" I asked.

"Sure did."

"Can we read it?"

"Not a chance," said Leslie. "I don't want you getting big heads. But I promise you that it was all quite complimentary."

After a few more congratulatory words from Leslie, and a bunch more celebratory hugs with TJ in the lobby, it was time for them to head home and me to go upstairs.

Mom screamed when I showed her the email. Like, literally screamed. In a good way. She hugged me tight and then screamed again.

"A statue? A statue! My baby wrote a report so good they might make a statue of it! Oh, I'm so proud of you, honey!" She kissed me on the head and squeezed me again before letting go. She printed out the email and put it on the fridge. Then we went out to Joe & Pat's pizza to celebrate over gooey cheese and crackably thin crust, where she told the server and anyone else who would listen about the statue. I wasn't sure if they believed us, but I got a free Italian ice out of it, so it was hard to complain.

It wasn't long until we found out who our competition was, or at least some of it.

When we walked into Watras's class the next day, the whiteboard was more obnoxious than ever. The words

WATRAS'S WINNERS were still on top, but now, in even larger letters, Watras had added BOROUGH-WIDE FINALISTS! Worse, he had printed out an oversized photograph of Borough Hall to put behind Erik and Dan's picture of Henry Hudson so that it looked like Hudson was already standing there, surveying "his" bay and peeking into the distance at "his" river. And just in case anyone had happened not to notice it, Watras started the class with a round of applause for Erik and Dan.

"You're nearly there, boys," he said. "Just three more projects to face. And, honestly, I can't see anyone outdoing Henry Hudson."

"He's not from Staten Island," Abe whispered.

"He's not even from New York," Josh whispered back.

Watras cleared his throat and scanned his eyes across the room for moving lips.

I wondered whether Watras knew we were finalists too. I didn't think so, given that he didn't give us any especially evil looks. If TJ and I were a different kind of people—you know, the kind with untearable skin and unbreakable bones—we might have made an announcement right then and there. Instead, I imagined the look on his face, as well as Dan's and Erik's, when we showed up to the judging event. I struggled to keep my laugh to myself.

I couldn't wait for them to find out they hadn't heard the last of Alice Austen.

CHAPTER FOURTEEN

"Did you tell her yet?" TJ asked as we threw the tennis ball back and forth in the churchyard that weekend, Nacious running between us . . . and after the ball when we missed, which was often.

"Did I tell who what?"

TJ put their hand on their hip and twirled their head in full diva fashion. "Did you tell the Queen of England about your new app idea? What do you think? Did you tell Jess about the statue judging? It's next Friday."

I shook my head.

"You're still not talking to her?"

"I don't know if she wants to talk to me." And even if she did, it wasn't going to be easy. Or fun.

"Why not?"

"It's been weeks and she hasn't said anything."

"Well, neither have you."

"Yeah, but she's the grown-up."

My own words echoed back at me and bounced off the phrase *chosen family* that had been clogging the thought lines of my mind. I don't know why it suddenly made sense to me then, but it did, and it took over my brain. Which is why when TJ tossed the ball my way, I didn't even think to catch it. It was aimed pretty well, at least for us, and landed right behind my feet. Nacious dove between my legs, squirming and tripping me in the process. I landed on the ground, the pug scrambling for the tennis ball under my butt, as I realized that Jess and I weren't best friends. We were something else, something more. Something I wasn't ready to lose.

By the time we were walking back to my building, I was sure enough about how I felt to say something to TJ. "I'm gonna text her."

"Finally!" they cried. "I mean, good for you!" They hugged my arms so tightly to my sides that I couldn't hug back. "I hope it goes well."

At the door to Leslie's apartment, I handed over Nacious's leash, and Leslie invited me in for some lemonade.

"No thanks."

She frowned.

"I gotta go upstairs and text Jess."

"Oh!" Her eyes popped open with surprise. "In that case, forget I offered. Go! Do your thing!"

I was so energized that I ran up the four flights of stairs to my apartment. I rushed into my room, took out my phone, opened a new message—and stared at it.

I spent the next ten minutes writing the shortest, hardest, least creative text ever, and another ten minutes getting up the nerve to send it.

SamSaysSo: I miss you

I stared at my phone, rereading that short little sentence, then forced myself to put it down and get out my science textbook. Maybe she was changing Evie. Maybe she was at the grocery store. Maybe Val wasn't teaching that weekend and they were spending the day together. Should I have just said hi? Should I have told her about the statue finals? I read the same introductory paragraph about plant cell structure eight times before my phone buzzed.

JessSinger: I miss you too, Sam

SamSaysSo: can we talk sometime?

JessSinger: I'd like that. what are you doing now?

SamSaysSo: failing to concentrate on my homework

JessSinger: I just made a berry crisp

SamSaysSo: I'll be right down

If we were going to have a hard conversation, my favorite non-chocolate-based dessert should be involved. I put on my fuzzy slippers, ran downstairs, and froze at the door. Was it okay to go in? What if it was locked and Jess heard me try to turn the doorknob? I decided to knock.

"Come on in!"

Inside, it smelled like berries and browning sugar. Jess and Evie were on the floor in the living room. I joined them and focused my attention on Evie. I tickled her tummy and let her hold my finger in her teeny-tiny hand.

I wasn't looking at Jess, but I knew she was looking at me, at least some of the time. I stayed quiet long enough to know that she was waiting for me to start. I knew what I needed to say, and the words scraped their way off my tongue.

"I'm sorry."

"Thank you, Sam. It's good to hear that."

The next words came more easily, and I felt my shoulders lift. "You were right. We aren't best friends. You knew it and I didn't. You must think I'm an idiot."

Jess's eyes bore into me as she formed her thoughts.

"First"—her voice grew sharp, just as I had feared—"don't tell me what I think. Second, don't use ableist language. And third, don't insult someone I love!"

"Wait, what?"

"Don't use the i-word."

"No, the other thing."

"I love you, Sam."

"I love you too, Jess."

I practically jumped on her to give her a huge hug, and she hugged me just as tightly, our bellies touching. It was even better than a belly bump.

"Berry crisp?" she asked. "It's still warm."

"Yes, please."

"With vanilla ice cream?"

"Are rainbows happy?"

Jess tilted her head to the side. "You know, I have no idea if rainbows are happy. I mean, I don't think they have consciousness, so can they really be said to be happy?"

"I meant yes, Jess."

"I know." Jess smiled.

It was amazing how quickly the tension melted between us. Or maybe it had already melted weeks ago and I was too busy holing myself up in an emotional freezer to notice.

Jess made us bowls of deliciousness in the kitchen and came back to sit in her favorite chair. I took a seat on the couch across from her. The first bite was an explosion of flavors, textures, and temperatures. I could hear the sugary crisp layer crackle as I broke through it with my spoon. Add in the swirl of warmth from the berries and the chill from the vanilla ice cream and it was more than a dessert—it was an experience. Jess's berry crisp with ice cream made me understand why cartoon characters floated toward pies when their wafting scent formed a beckoning finger.

A few bites later, Jess spoke. "I'm sorry. It's my fault too. I should have said something sooner. I knew it was going to come up at some point."

My face crumpled, and my cheeks felt as warm as berry crisp. "That day we went to the library."

"Yeah, that was part of it. But it's been something we've needed to talk about for a while. When we first met and you called me your 'friend downstairs like you,' it was sweet. And when you were six, that was a good enough description of our relationship."

"Wow," I said, "I just realized I've known you half my life."

"Six years ago, I was already out of college." Jess laughed.

"Oh." I hadn't really thought about how much life Jess had lived before we ever met.

"Which isn't bad, but it's why we're not best friends. Or, well, a sign of it anyway."

"Leslie told me about chosen family, and I was wondering if maybe we could be that instead."

"Sam, dear, I would be honored to be part of your chosen fam."

"What about Evie?"

"Her too, of course."

"And Val?"

"Well, I can't speak for them directly, but I'm pretty sure you're stuck with all three of us."

Maybe it was just the berry crisp, but talking with Jess about this stuff wasn't all that bad. It was way better than thinking about talking with her about it. I took another bite, trying to savor it, but enjoying each mouthful too much not to follow it up with another. Besides, the ice cream was melting.

"Funny that you made berry crisp on the first day that we've talked in over a month."

"Well, it's not exactly a coincidence." Jess shrugged. "I ran into Leslie in the hallway this morning and she gave a hint that you might reach out. I didn't have any chocolate around, but I had these berries in the freezer, so I took a chance."

"Did she say why?"

"No, but she seemed pleased with herself and said something about putting a fire under your butt."

I laughed. Nacious and the tennis ball had done it before Leslie could try.

"Do *you* know why?"

"I think so." I said. "Remember that statue of Alice Austen that TJ and I were working on?"

"I very much do. It was the last thing we talked about."

"And then you asked Leslie to enter it into the contest."

"I did," said Jess. "I hope you don't mind. I thought you'd appreciate making the committee learn a little bit about Alice. I figured I'd tell you about it once we were talking again. Why, did Leslie say something?"

"No," I said, "Judy did."

"Who's Judy?"

"Judy Roberts, president of the Staten Island Historians Association."

"Wait—what? Do you mean—?"

"No, I don't mean. I kind."

Jess grinned. That was one of the first puns I had ever made, and we used to say it all the time to each other.

"Did Alice Austen win the contest?"

"Not yet, but she's a finalist, and there are only four of those."

"Congratulations!" said Jess.

"We're going to present our project to the judges next Friday."

"Wow, it's been a busy month for you."

"Busy, but also, I missed you," I said.

"I missed you too, Sam." Jess put her arm around my shoulder and squeezed me into her pillowy body. I felt safe and protected, and it struck me as silly that I had ever thought of Jess as *just* a best friend. She was so much more than that. She was part of my queer family.

"If you wanted, you could maybe come on Friday," I offered.

"There's nowhere I'd rather be," said Jess.

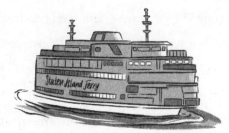

CHAPTER FIFTEEN

Friday was the slowest day in the history of school, and the minutes of Watras's class oozed by like cold honey that won't come out of the jar. He reminded us at both the start and end of the lesson that Erik, Dan, and the other finalists would be presenting to the Historians Association at the St. George Library that evening and said he would give extra credit to anyone who attended and wrote a paragraph about the event.

"Do you think he'll give *us* extra credit for being finalists?" TJ asked me in the hallway after class finally ended.

I snorted. "I don't think so. But you can ask. He'll be there tonight."

I thought TJ was going to choke they laughed so hard. And I made sure not to look their way in math class, because one or both of us would have lost it. Our nervousness made everything funnier.

After school, we headed first to my apartment and then to TJ's to change. TJ, of course, insisted on dressing our best for the judges, but we couldn't wear our presentation outfits at school and risk ruining the surprise for Erik, Dan, and, most of all, Watras. TJ wouldn't look that out of the ordinary, besides the extra-fancy shoes, but me in a collared shirt instead of a T-shirt with a cartoon or writing on it? That would stand out.

We had decided last week to wear the first outfits we planned for the presentation back in Watras's class—me in my black polo shirt with the tiny polka dots, black stretch pants, and sparkly sneakers, TJ in their black button-down with white piping, black velveteen pants, and oxford shoes. Well, TJ decided, and I'd had no reason to disagree. TJ even went out to their dad's garden, plucked a daisy, and pinned it to their shirt.

"You two look amazing," said TJ's dad from the kitchen counter, where he was chopping carrots. He was a tall, thin man and wore a red apron that said LOVE IS THE REVOLUTION. FEED IT WELL.

"Thank you, TJ's dad."

"Please, Sam, I've told you: Call me Marcus. Or Chef."

"OK, the Littles' dad!" I said.

TJ's dad shook his head.

"Are you almost ready to go?" TJ asked.

"Just tossing a few veggies into the pot so that we'll have

dinner when we get back, if you think you'll be wanting to eat tonight. Why don't you gather your siblings? It'll take them a few minutes to get ready anyway."

"Just the Littles, right?"

"You got it. Miles and Parker are hanging out with friends, but they both know to be at the library by six and your mom is driving there directly from work."

Two shoe searches and three chopped potatoes later, we were out the door. I texted Mom and Jess, who met us outside our building, and all seven of us walked down the hill together, like a mini parade. The Littles kept running ahead of us until TJ's dad told them to stop. Then they would race back, loop around behind us, and take off again.

Val drove Evie and Leslie, and they met us at the front of the library. TJ's granddad from New Jersey had driven in too and was waiting there in his pin-striped suit, feathered fedora, and silver-tipped cane.

"Gramps! You made it!" TJ gave their granddad a huge, back-slapping hug.

"Let me look at you!" He motioned for TJ to give a spin. TJ was happy to do so.

"Snappy, snappy!" TJ's granddad said.

"You too, Gramps!"

"You look pretty great yourself," said TJ's dad to me.

"Thanks, but fashion is TJ's thing."

The adults introduced each other and shook hands and milled about until Leslie asked, "Are we ready to go in? My knees say it's time to sit."

"Yours and mine both," said TJ's granddad.

"Then let's do this thing!" TJ looked over at me, with their most *ready to go onstage and be phenomenal* grin.

My belly flopped, and I suddenly realized that I was nervous. Very nervous. Reading a report to some seventh graders was one thing. But to adult judges? Historians, even? Plus Watras, Dan, and Erik would be there. Goose bumps ran up my arm to my neck. I shuddered.

But then I remembered that I was surrounded by my mom, my chosen queer family, my best friend, and their family. It was like a web of connection. It made me think about that old book about the spider who could write words in her webs. If I were a spider like that, I would write *FAMILY*.

"Sam?" asked Leslie.

"With you all here? I'm ready for anything."

I marched up the steep steps and into the cool, dark air of the library. Jess spoke to the librarian at the front desk, who directed us toward the stairs, where we found signs that guided us to a large meeting room. The room was filling with people, mostly adults, and the hum of their voices. Twelve rows of twelve folding chairs each had been set up.

Some people were already sitting, but most were standing, chatting with one another.

A tall person with a bright blue blazer, chunky necklace, and feathered white-blond hair approached us with a warm smile and a handshake. "Hi, I'm Judy Roberts, she/her, president of the Staten Island Historians Association. Are you two finalists?"

TJ spoke first. "We sure are. I'm TJ Williams and this is Sam Marino. We both use they."

"We did our project on Alice Austen," I added.

"Of course, of course. It was a fantastic report, and I look forward to your presentation. You're scheduled to go last. Is that okay?"

"Great!" TJ and I said together. The less time Watras, Dan, and Erik knew we were finalists, the better.

Judy introduced us to a few other members of the board, who were gathered around a large table with a thick blue tablecloth at the side of the stage. Then she let us go back to our group with a "Congratulations and best of luck!"

Our cheer team filled half of two rows midway back, including TJ's mom, who had arrived while we were meeting the judges. TJ's family was in one row, with their mom and dad separating the Littles, plus TJ's granddad and two empty seats for the Bigs when they arrived. In front of them were

Mom, Leslie, Jess, Val with Evie in their lap, and two empty seats on the aisle for TJ and me.

"So you can get up easily when it's your turn," Hannah, one of the Littles, explained with a proud grin.

"Good thinking!" said TJ.

TJ spotted Erik and Dan before I did, near the front. Watras was with them, along with four adults we assumed were their parents. We had almost twice that many people, not including kids (not even the Bigs!).

"There's an awful lot of us," I said. "Do you think they'll notice us?"

"Nah," said TJ. "This circus of ours is camouflage, and more people are coming in all the time."

"Good point." I looked around the crowd. There must have been over a hundred people in the room. Mostly adults, but I spotted Josh and Abe from school. I pointed them out to TJ.

"See? Even if they do see us, they'll just think we're here for the extra credit."

We weren't sitting long before a slight person with balding black hair and an angular jaw approached us with a hand outstretched. They wore a white shirt, gray blazer, and a single pink triangle earring. "TJ and Sam, I take it?"

We nodded.

"I'm Gabe. He/him. I'm on the judging committee. I

missed you when Judy brought you by the judges' table."

"It's nice to meet you." TJ smiled in that way that puts a twinkle in their eye. I tried my best to look confident.

Gabe gave us each a firm-but-not-squeezing handshake. "Is one of these fine adults here your teacher? Or rather, Ms. Leslie Hansen, I should say. I understand that she's not your teacher."

I gasped. "Is that a problem? She *is* our teacher . . . just not in school."

"Oh, oh, not to worry. The committee wasn't expecting it, but it's in line with the requirements. To be honest, I thought we should accept a letter from any nonrelative adult, but some of the committee members have been . . . shall we say . . . less than open to updating the rulebook. Anyway, I wanted to thank her for entering your project."

Leslie was in a deep discussion about knee pain with TJ's granddad, but we got her attention and Gabe shook her hand.

"It is a pleasure to meet you, Ms. Hansen," said Gabe. "As a gay teacher, I can't even imagine what it was like teaching back when you did."

"We got by," said Leslie. "And please, call me Leslie. Only straight people call me Ms. Hansen." She winked at him.

"Well, Leslie, your letter was inspiring, and we figured that if these kids inspired you, they must truly be something. And I have to say, the committee has appreciated learning more about Alice Austen. We all knew who she was, of course, but I was surprised how many of our members didn't know she was part of the rainbow."

"If you want to help the rest of Staten Island learn about our community, you know how to vote." TJ gave their best shrug-n-grin.

"Before we know it, you'll be running City Council!" Gabe laughed. "I'd better get going, before I get accused of playing favorites."

As he left, TJ and I both heard him mutter, "It's about time someone else had a favorite." Either Gabe wasn't very careful or he wanted us to hear him.

I scanned the room again and couldn't see Dan, Erik, or Watras. I hoped that was a good thing. Still, I kept checking behind me, half expecting to find them there with diamond-sharp piercing glares, but all that I could see was a growing crowd. Some wore dark suits and blazers, the kind of outfit that TJ calls *a waste of dressing up*, but a few wore bright colors and snazzy patterns, the kind of outfit that TJ calls *a visual song*. There were also plenty of people in everyday jeans and T-shirts.

The Bigs, Miles and Parker, arrived right at six p.m., and it was good that we had saved them seats, because by that time, there were about a dozen people standing at the back of the room. Who knew so many people wanted to watch some middle school students fight over a statue?

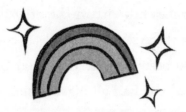

CHAPTER SIXTEEN

By the time the secretary of the Staten Island Historians Association approached the microphone at the front of the room, the place was packed. She welcomed us and told us about the association before introducing Judy Roberts.

"I am both delighted and honored to welcome all four pairs of finalists to today's event," said Judy Roberts. "I've spoken with you individually, but once again, congratulations to you all. The judges have already reviewed your statue images and your written reports and found them to be exemplary, which is why you were invited here today. The finalists have been asked to say a few additional words about their choices, and then the committee will vote. So, rather than drag things out, I'd like to welcome Reese Webber and Kelsey Ingram."

The first pair of kids looked really nervous. They were

both pale white with thin white-blond hair and freckles, one about three inches taller than the other. They looked like they might have been siblings, or at least cousins. They spoke quietly about Robert Gould Shaw, a white Union officer from the Civil War who led an all-Black regiment of soldiers and advocated for their equal treatment by the Army. An image of the proposed statue was projected on a screen to their side, showing a mustachioed, slim man standing at attention in his uniform. His regiment was nowhere in sight.

While the audience clapped and the judges wrote notes, I heard Parker say to Miles behind us, "So a white guy makes a bunch of Black guys fight and he's the one they want to make a statue of?"

"Typical," Miles said.

Judy Roberts introduced the next contestants to the stage, Cherrie Davis and Angela Moraga.

"We believe Staten Island deserves a statue of Audre Lorde," said Cherrie, a Black kid with short, natural hair and a black vest over a rainbow T-shirt. They raised a fist along with Angela, a Latinx kid with rosy, rounded cheeks and a neatly folded purple handkerchief hanging out of the pocket of their crisp white shirt.

"She was an amazing person who called herself a '*black, lesbian, mother, warrior, poet,*'" Cherrie continued. "And she lived right here on Staten Island, in Stapleton."

"Audre Lorde lived here," Val whispered behind me. "I had no idea."

I looked back at Val, who was staring with their mouth slightly open, as though they had just realized that stop signs and stoplights are both red on purpose.

"Looks like Professor Cutepants gets to do some research," Jess whispered.

Val beamed.

Behind the finalists was their statue proposal: Audre Lorde holding a pencil in one hand and lowering her glasses with the other as she peered at whatever was in front of her. They told us she lived at 207 St. Paul's Avenue from 1972 to 1987, when she wrote her most important essays, including "The Master's Tools Will Never Dismantle the Master's House." A section of the audience to our left broke into cheers at the essay's name, probably the presenters' families. Cherrie and Angela raised their fists again and stepped down from the stage.

"If we don't win, I sure hope they do," said TJ.

"Me too!" I agreed. Audre Lorde never lived in my building, but anyone who made Val that excited had to be amazing.

"I think Cherrie and Angela might be queer. Or nonbinary. Or both."

"You get that feeling too?"

After that, Erik and Dan were called up to the stage to give their presentation on Henry Hudson. They used the version of their picture Watras had hung in class, so it looked like Hudson was already standing in front of Borough Hall. They talked proudly and smiled as if they had won, but I was barely listening. It was as though they didn't matter anymore. I wanted to learn more about Audre Lorde, not to mention Angela and Cherrie.

And then it was our turn. Watras, Erik, and Dan all whipped their heads around the moment our names were called. Once we got to the front, I could see Erik and Dan whispering to their families, probably telling them who we were. Watras was, for once in his life, completely speechless. His mouth even hung open like a cartoon character's, and his eyebrows could have flown off his head. I looked out into the audience, but I couldn't see Cherrie and Angela. The only reason I could find our group was by the two empty seats we had left behind. They were the only empty seats in the place.

TJ spoke first. "When we proposed Alice Austen for this statue, our teacher said it didn't represent Staten Island. But Staten Island is a place with lots of kinds of people, straight and queer; men, women, and nonbinary folk. And it always has been and it always will be. The image that we picked, called *The Darned Club*, shows that. We want people coming off the ferry to see Alice and her three friends having the time of their lives with one another."

They pointed at their drawing projected behind us, four

women from Staten Island who loved each other. Then it was my turn to speak. I could feel Watras, Erik, and Dan staring at me, but I didn't look their way. Instead, I looked back to where Jess was waving Evie's tiny arm and our families beamed with joy and pride. I saw Leslie nod, like she knew the value of every word I was about to say. And then I spotted Cherrie and Angela, who met my eye contact with big grins and four thumbs-up.

"There's a statue I can see from my bedroom window. It doesn't look very big from where I am, but it's over three hundred feet tall. It's the Statue of Liberty. Liberty means freedom, including the freedom to be yourself. Alice Austen believed in this freedom, and lived and loved the way she wanted for most of her life. This statue will help LGBTQIAP+ people on Staten Island and everywhere know that they have the right to be who they are."

The audience applauded, we took our seats, and the secretary returned to the microphone.

"We'd like to thank all our finalists for their thoughtful words. The judges will now confer, and we'll announce our winner in about fifteen minutes. Don't go far!"

The room buzzed with excitement and congratulations. The Bigs disappeared the moment the secretary stopped speaking, and the Littles went off running in between clusters of people, but Mom's, Leslie's, Val's, Jess's, and TJ's parents' and granddad's words toppled over each other as they told us how amazing we'd been.

"Leslie," Val asked, "did you know that the great Lorde lived on Staten Island?"

Leslie nodded. "I even met her a few times, and once we took the ferry home together after a talk she gave in Manhattan."

"Really?" Val looked impressed, as though they were practically standing in front of Audre Lorde herself. "I'd love to hear about that sometime."

"Me too," said Jess.

"And me!" I added.

"Can I join in?" asked TJ.

"Of course!" said Leslie.

"Maybe we can start an intergenerational queer share space!" said Val.

"A what queer what what?" I asked.

"Like we could all get together and talk about what it was like to be queer in the past?" asked TJ.

"That," said Val, "and also what it's like to be queer now at different ages."

"I could use some hip young friends to catch me up on the latest," said Leslie. "I haven't learned a dance since the Macarena!"

While Mom, Val, and Jess were still laughing and trying to remember the hand motions to that old dance, I scanned the room. I spotted Watras over at the judges' table and nudged TJ with my elbow.

"What do you want to bet he's complaining about our project?" said TJ.

"He might be trying to convince them to vote for Erik and Dan's."

"Like that's so much better."

"Either way, Judy's not having it."

We watched as she shooed him away with her hand like a neighbor who had run out of candy and didn't think kids over the age of ten should be trick-or-treating anyway. It was so funny that TJ and I kept imitating it and cracking up until the lights blinked and an announcement came over the library speakers that the winning entry would be named momentarily.

Once nearly everyone had taken their seats, Judy Roberts stepped up to the microphone.

"Wow!" she said. "Wow wow wow! Let's have another round of applause for these fantastic young folks who have presented tonight." The audience clapped and cheered. I was holding TJ's hand too tight to let go, but we tried clapping with their left hand and my right, and it worked. Sort of.

"All eight of you, and your families and friends, should be very proud. You have done great jobs, and you will all receive lifetime memberships to the Historians Association.

However, Borough Hall is only providing one plinth, and so the judges here had to make a tough decision.

"First runners-up, and recipients of fifty dollars each, goes to Cherrie Davis and Angela Moraga, for their suggestion of Audre Lorde. Ms. Lorde is an important figure in literature, and we will be seeking out future opportunities to recognize her connection to Staten Island."

The audience clapped again, more loudly this time, with cheers from their section of the crowd and a loud "Go, Audre!" from Val.

"And now, for the winners of tonight's competition, recipients of one hundred dollars apiece, and, more importantly, designers of Staten Island's upcoming statue at Borough Hall . . ."

TJ squeezed my hand. I squeezed back.

"Sam Marino and TJ Williams, for Alice Austen and *The Darned Club*. Ms. Austen was chosen for her local importance and lifelong island residency, and the statue design representing her with three other women in such an affectionate pose makes it both about Alice and about something much bigger than Alice. While the modern LGBTQIAP+ community and its language didn't exist then as it does today, she, and many others, found ways to be connected. Congratulations to Sam and TJ! Come on up here!"

I looked at TJ, who looked at me. We stared at each other, eyes wide.

"Go on, go!" said Leslie. "This is the moment you worked for! Take your kudos!"

I could hear the ocean in my ears, or maybe it was the bay, as we headed up and shook the judges' hands and the crowd broke into applause and cheers.

"Thank you all for attending tonight's event. Have a safe trip home, and if you are on our mailing list, we'll keep you updated on the statue's progress. Good night." Judy stepped away from the podium.

Gabe approached us as the murmurs of the released audience filled the room. "Congratulations again . . . and thank you!"

"Thank us?" I said. "Thank *you*. You're the ones who picked our entry."

"And you're the ones who gave us such a good entry to choose." He looked left and right before covering his mouth on one side and half whispering, "Do you know how many statues of Henry Hudson we had to go through?"

"There's already a statue of Henry Hudson in the Bronx, and that colonizer doesn't need another one," said TJ.

"No kidding." Gabe looked like he wanted to say more, but by that time, a circle of adults three people deep had formed, wanting to congratulate us, thank us, and wish us well.

One person would leave and another two would join, mingling among each other as they waited their turn to talk to two kids. Handshake after handshake, and far too many palms on shoulders, as the accolades piled up. Eventually, the crowd began to shrink as people peeled off after their donation of appreciation, and we began to see individuals in the smattering of people who remained.

Two of those figures were Cherrie and Angela.

"Congratulations," said Cherrie.

"Thanks," said TJ. "You too. I'd never heard of Audre Lorde before. She sounds amazing."

"She is. And we didn't know about Alice Austen," said Angela. "If we didn't win, we're glad you did. That picture of them hugging is awesome. I just know I'm going to smile every time I see it."

"I'm glad you four are still here." It was Gabe again. "I was wondering whether you'd be interested in working with me on a project."

"A project?" All four of us said it at once, and then laughed.

"Well, you see, the contract we have with Borough Hall only provides one plinth. But I was thinking that with the right fundraising plan, and some willing young activists, we could raise the money for a second statue. What do you say?"

"I know where we can get our first two hundred dollars from," said TJ, "if it's all right with Sam to use our prize money."

"It's perfect!" I exclaimed.

"We've got another hundred dollars!" said Angela.

"That is generous of you, but this project would cost much, much more than that, so we'd be looking into getting a grant. But your proposal, Angela and Cherrie, and a letter of support from you, Sam and TJ, would both be quite helpful in showing the foundation the importance of our work. Let me check in with some folks and get back to you. It's been a pleasure to meet all four of you . . . and once again, congratulations."

We grinned at each other. None of us knew what to say, but it was less awkward than you might think, and we stayed that way until a deep voice called over to Angela and Cherrie that it was time to go. We exchanged hugs and promised to stay in touch. If Gabe meant what he said, we certainly would.

After that, it was just our group. Mom, my best friend and their family, my chosen queer family, and my lesbian mentor. Evie might turn out to be part of the queer community too, and she'll be lucky to have so much connection to her community so young. I hope I get to be one of her queer mentors. And even if she's not queer, straight kids get to have queer mentors too, I guess.

Everyone in both our families gave TJ and me giant hugs and high fives along with congratulations. Everyone except

Jess and me, of course, who celebrated with not one, not two, but three giant belly bumps in a row.

"Belly power!" we yelled, not caring who saw or heard us.

Before we left, I took one more look at TJ's drawing, which was still projected on the wall. I'd seen it a bunch of times, and the photo it came from, but I wanted to see it again now that I knew it was going to really become a statue. The women were looking into each other's eyes like there was no one but the four of them, and time didn't exist at all. They would be standing in bronze in the present, but they would also be in their time over a hundred years ago and would still be standing there in over a hundred years, gazing endlessly at each other's beauty and wonder.

AUTHOR'S NOTE

Hi! Thanks for reading about Sam, TJ, and, of course, Alice Austen. I had a great time writing this story, and I hope you enjoyed it. Before you go, I'd like to tell you a little more about why I wrote it and how it connects with my own queer history.

I grew up on Staten Island, the "kid sibling" borough of New York City. What's more, I grew up at 141 St. Mark's Place, Apartment 4-E. I still hear it in my head with the same singsong Sam and I both used to memorize where we lived. (I gave Sam the honor of living right in 5-C, Alice and Gertrude's old place. Jess, Val, and Evie are in my old apartment.) I used to see the Statue of Liberty and the Manhattan skyline outside my bedroom window, just like Sam does, and I used to take the ferry to get to the rest of the city, sometimes even on the boat named the *Alice Austen*.

Yep, Alice Austen is real, and she really was a lesbian. There's no documentation that she used that exact word, but her partnership with Gertrude Tate spanned fifty years. Language changes over time, and while the word *lesbian* was first used in the 1800s, it wasn't a term many people called themselves with pride until the gay liberation and feminist movements of the 1960s and 1970s.

There really was a Ms. Hansen who lived in my building,

too, though she had a canary, not a pug, and I have no reason to think she was a lesbian, other than the fact that anyone in my building could have been LGBTQIAP+. Maybe the woman and her kid who I "babysat" for, or the sisters who went to Curtis High School across the street, or the two women who lived upstairs with their dogs. Actually, those last two I did later learn were partners.

Why hadn't I grown up knowing that they were a couple like my parents were? I don't think anything was actively hidden from me, but I'm pretty sure the language was coded and I certainly had been primed to expect heterosexuality. I hope this book helps show that queer and trans people are everywhere, come from everywhere, and have always been everywhere. If you live on a block with a dozen or more people, odds are high that not all of them are straight and cisgender.

Even though I grew up knowing about Alice Austen as a photographer and local celebrity with a house that had been turned into a museum, I didn't learn that she was a lesbian until I was in college. Imagine my surprise in finding her name in a book on queer history. I ordered *Alice's World* by Ann Novotny through my school's interlibrary loan system and pored over the pages, much like Sam and TJ do.

I saw the young eccentric people Alice surrounded herself with—the women who rode bicycles before that was common and, of course, the statue-inspiring *The Darned Club*. And like Sam, I noticed that Alice and Gertrude had spent a few years near the end of their lives in the same building I grew up in. I had never felt more connected to the past. I even wrote an article about my dive into queer history for my university's LGB Center newsletter. (Well, that was the name at the time. It's been the LGBT Center for twenty years now. Just more of that changing language in action.)

All the queer and trans history in this book is real, and I encourage you to seek out more information on your own, especially since most schools never talk about it. *Pride: Celebrating Diversity & Community* by Robin Stevenson is a great book to learn about LGBTQIAP+ people and communities over time, and *The Stonewall Riots: Coming Out in the Streets* by Gayle E. Pitman covers the period leading up to the modern queer rights movement in more detail.

The lack of statues representing women is also a real problem, including in New York City. Until recently, only five of the one hundred and fifty statues of historical people around the city represented women: Gertrude Stein, Eleanor Roosevelt, Harriet Tubman, Joan of Arc, and Golda Meir. In 2020, Central Park got its first statue to honor women, with Sojourner Truth, Susan B. Anthony, and Elizabeth Cady Stanton sharing a table and conversation.

She Built NYC, a public-arts campaign, is working to

double the number of statues honoring real women throughout the city: Rep. Shirley Chisholm in Brooklyn, Billie Holiday in Queens, Elizabeth Jennings Graham in Manhattan, Dr. Helen Rodríguez Trías in the Bronx, Katherine Walker on Staten Island, and Marsha P. Johnson and Sylvia Rivera (together, of course!) in Greenwich Village (Manhattan), home of the Stonewall Inn. And they don't plan to stop there. Neither Alice Austen nor Audre Lorde are currently on She Built NYC's list of statues-to-be, but maybe they will be someday.

The Staten Island Historians Association is fictional, as well as the statue contest, but I would like to thank the real Staten Island Historical Society for preserving local history, including many of Alice Austen's photographs, and for giving us permission to reproduce several of them for you here.

And of course, I want to thank and celebrate my queer chosen family, mentors, friends, and community—young and old; past, present, and future. We may not be related by blood, but we are connected by so much more. I would be lost without you. Sparkle on!

The Darned Club by Alice Austen. This photo features Alice with her good friends (from left to right) Trude Eccleston, Julia (Marsh) Lord, and Sue Ripley. According to the book *Alice's World* by Ann Novotny, the group was given the nickname "the Darned Club" by the young men of the neighborhood, who felt excluded by the women's close friendship. *From the collection of the Staten Island Historical Society.*

A photograph of Clear Comfort, Alice Austen's home for much of her life. If you look closely, you can see her grandfather sitting outside and a telescope used for stargazing. *From the collection of the New York Public Library.*

Portrait by Alice Austen of herself (left), Julia Martin (center), and Julia Bredt (right) dressed as men, "just for fun." *From the collection of the Staten Island Historical Society.*

Alice Austen took this while visiting with friends in Bethlehem, Pennsylvania. The woman seated at the table is Alice's friend Julia Bredt, and the others in the group are identified in the photographer's inscription as "Messrs Rawl, Ordway, Blunt, Buel, Gibson, and Maurice." *From the collection of the Staten Island Historical Society.*

Longtime companions Alice Austen and Gertrude Tate out for a row. Alice is standing, an oar in her hands and her cameras at her feet. Gertrude smiles in the back of the boat. *From the collection of the Staten Island Historical Society.*

ABOUT THE AUTHOR

Alex Gino is the author of the middle grade novels *Rick*; *You Don't Know Everything, Jilly P!*; and the Stonewall Award–winning *Melissa*, which was originally published as *George*. They love glitter, ice cream, gardening, awe-ful puns, and stories that reflect the complexity of being alive. For more information, visit alexgino.com.